BY THE LIGHT OF THE MOON

The Moonlight Breed 2

Gabrielle Evans

EROTIC ROMANCE

Siren Publishing, Inc.
www.SirenPublishing.com

A SIREN PUBLISHING BOOK
IMPRINT: Erotic Romance

BY THE LIGHT OF THE MOON
Copyright © 2011 by Gabrielle Evans

ISBN-10: 1-61034-477-4
ISBN-13: 978-1-61034-477-7

First Printing: March 2011

Cover design by Jinger Heaston
All cover art and logo copyright © 2011 by Siren Publishing, Inc.

Printed in the U.S.A.

PUBLISHER
Siren Publishing, Inc.
www.SirenPublishing.com

DEDICATION

To Sidney Octavian, for reminding me why I love my job so much, but mostly because he makes me smile.

BY THE LIGHT OF THE MOON

The Moonlight Breed 2

GABRIELLE EVANS

Chapter One

"Okay, everyone hide. Boston, you turn off the lights. Keeton just texted, and they're almost here." Braxton Carmichael ran about the room, tossing orders over his shoulder as he went.

Logan Cartwright glanced at his brother, Talon, and smiled. He was happy for their pack brother, Xander. Braxton was a good mate, and a good friend. All the guys adored him. Talon rolled his eyes, but even he smiled.

Logan sighed and wrapped an arm around his date's shoulders. He'd been seeing Mariah Bernini for a little over a month. She was a pretty girl, small, petite, with nice round breasts and long ebony curls. She exuded intelligence—well-educated and well-spoken—and the sex left him craving more.

She could also be clingy, needy, boring, and just a little creepy. Logan would catch her staring at him sometimes as if she wanted to eat him—not in the good, sexual kind of way either.

Add to that the fact that he couldn't scent her emotions. He had never met another person that he could not scent *something* from them. Hell, he hadn't even been able to smell her tears when she cried at that chick flick she dragged him to see.

He knew he needed to break it off soon. Maybe they could talk after their date later in the evening. Braxton would kill him if he caused drama during Xander's party. Though he didn't look forward to going to the theater with Mariah, she had already purchased the tickets. It would probably be a dickhead move to cancel at the last minute.

The room suddenly plunged into darkness, and Braxton hissed at everyone to be quiet and hide. Logan took Mariah's hand and pulled her into the kitchen with the majority of the other guests. He heard the crunch of tires against the gravel drive as Xander pulled up in front of the house.

Two sets of footsteps reached Logan's ears, along with Xander's deep, rolling laughter, and another voice, slightly higher pitched. *Was that a giggle?* The sound shot a jolt of electricity straight to Logan's groin, causing him to groan out loud.

Mariah leaned up, pressing her lips to his ear, and whispered, "You okay, honey?"

Am I okay? He didn't think so, but he nodded and gave her a weak smile. Shifting away from his date, he hoped she wouldn't notice the sudden bulge in his jeans.

The front door opened, and the lights came on. Shouts of "Surprise!" echoed throughout the house. Boston and Jackson came forward, carrying an enormous cake, and everyone laughed and jeered as Xander blushed a brilliant red.

He grabbed his mate around the waist and planted a searing kiss on his lips. He looked deep into Braxton's eyes, smiling like a fool. "I love you, baby."

Braxton grinned back just as dreamily. "Love you back."

Logan smiled, but inside, something ached. God, he wanted that—wanted someone to look at him as if he was the most important person on earth. He knew Mariah enjoyed his company, maybe even cared for him, but he just couldn't see a future with her.

He clamped down on a sigh. The day belonged to Xander, and

Logan would support his family any way he could. Talon may be his only blood relation in the pack, but he considered each member his brother—his family.

* * * *

Keeton stumbled backward, his arms abruptly full of a very tipsy Braxton. "Thank you, thank you, thank you, Kee!" Braxton sang as he wrapped his arms around Keeton's neck and kissed him soundly on the mouth.

Keeton laughed, gently pushing his friend away. "You're very welcome, but I've grown quite attached to my balls, so maybe you should go find your man. Yes?"

Braxton just giggled, grabbing Keeton's hand and pulling him through the throng of people. "There's someone I want you to meet. I still can't believe, out of all the times you've been here, you guys keep managing to miss each other."

Keeton laughed and allowed Braxton to pull him along as he snaked his way through the crowd.

"I smell him. Where the hell is he?" Braxton lifted his nose and sniffed the air.

Keeton shook his head. He was still adjusting to his best friend's newfound abilities. He didn't mind, and Braxton hadn't changed much, but it still weirded him out when Braxton sniffed him. Mostly, he felt happy for his friend. He had found his true love, his mate, his missing half. He looked happier than Keeton had ever seen him.

"Aha!" Braxton cried. He tugged on Keeton's hand and led him across the yard to a group of men standing watch over the grill. Keeton rolled his eyes. He'd never understood why it always took at least three men to work a grill. Apparently, beer and an overabundance of testosterone were the secret ingredients for a great burger.

He recognized Talon and Jackson immediately, but he didn't

know the third man standing with them. The stranger stood almost a whole head taller than his own five-foot-seven, and Keeton had no problem making out the rippling cords of muscles under the tight white T-shirt. He licked his lips. He really hoped he was about to make this gorgeous creatures' acquaintance.

"Logan," Braxton called, walking right up to Keeton's new wet dream. The man turned, grinning broadly at them.

Keeton felt his heart do a double beat, and his stomach made a slow roll. He suddenly couldn't breathe. The most beautiful ice blue eyes he had ever seen pinned him in place with the intensity of their gaze. Short, blond hair stuck out in gelled spikes, and the stubble along the man's jaw looked sexy as hell.

Where just a second before, Keeton had been fantasizing about getting his hands all over that sun-kissed, golden skin, he suddenly felt very shy—a whole new experience for him.

"Logan, I'd like for you to *finally* meet Keeton Taylor." Braxton turned his attention to Keeton. "Kee, this is Logan Cartwright."

Logan held his hand out, giving Keeton a sexy smile. "It's so nice to finally meet you. I've heard a lot about you from the guys." Logan's voice sounded low and sultry, and set Keeton's blood boiling.

"I hope it's all been good." He smiled shyly as he shook Logan's hand.

"Oh yes, and now I see that it was all true, as well." Logan stepped closer, still holding on to Keeton's hand. He bent down, whispering into Keeton's ear, "You are absolutely gorgeous, baby."

Keeton shuddered at the raw desire in Logan's voice. This beautiful, godlike creature thought *him* gorgeous? He couldn't move, couldn't speak. Damn, he could barely breathe. All he knew in that moment was that he wanted Logan Cartwright like he'd never wanted anyone in all of his twenty-six years.

* * * *

Logan straightened slowly, making no move to hide the bulge pressing against his zipper. Keeton smelled amazing—like sugarcane and strawberries, and something floral...honeysuckle maybe. He wanted to find out if the little man tasted as good as he smelled. He wanted to run his tongue over every inch of Keeton's pale skin, starting with that sexy little ass of his.

Mine.

Oh yeah, Keeton belonged to him. After years of hoping, his destiny had just fallen into his lap. Logan felt it deep down to the core of his being. He felt...complete. His gums began to itch as they threatened to elongate, his stomach clenched, and everything melted away except for the man in front of him. He didn't even notice the strange looks that his brothers gave him. He stared into Keeton's deep blue eyes—eyes the color of the Caribbean waters. He was lost.

"Uh, Logan, we need to leave soon if we're going to make it to the theater on time."

Logan snapped his head up as reality rushed back to him. Clearing his throat, he took a step back, releasing his hold on Keeton's hand, and shook his head to clear the fog surrounding his brain. His gaze fell on Mariah, who stood a few steps away, looking from him to Keeton with a slight frown.

"Yes. Right. Okay...just give me a minute, please?" Logan turned to Keeton. "Can I speak to you alone for a second?"

Keeton didn't look at him, though. He watched Mariah with his brows drawn together.

Logan sighed. Why did he have to meet his mate now? Really, like fate couldn't have waited just one more day? Now it would appear as if he had dumped Mariah to be with Keeton. Fate could be a hateful bitch.

Logan cleared his throat again, bringing Keeton's attention back to him. "A minute alone? Please?" He tried to keep it casual, but even he could hear the pleading in his voice.

Keeton glanced at Mariah again before he nodded and followed Logan to the edge of the woods that bordered the backyard.

"Your girlfriend?" Keeton asked without preamble, his tone accusatory.

Logan took a deep breath, stalling as he gathered his thoughts. "I've been seeing her for a couple of weeks, but it's nothing serious. I don't belong to her."

Keeton gave him a confused look but didn't speak.

"Don't you feel it, angel? You belong to me, and I belong to you." He took Keeton's hand and brushed his thumb over the soft skin on his wrist. "Your heart is beating so fast, baby. I know you feel it."

Keeton dipped his head once. "Yes, I feel a…well, something. But from where I'm standing, you *do* belong to her."

Logan frowned. "No. I don't."

Keeton narrowed his eyes as he fisted his hands on his hips. "You should go before she starts to wonder what's taking you so long."

Logan sighed. "You're right, but I'll be back for you. Are you staying here tonight?"

Keeton tilted his head to the side as he considered him. "I'm staying the weekend actually. Jackson is supposed to teach me how to ride a motorcycle."

"Okay, baby. I'll see you tonight. We have lots of things to discuss." The first being that Keeton wasn't getting anywhere near one of those two-wheeled death machines. "Walk with me back to the house?"

God, he wanted Keeton. Everything about him made Logan hard as a rock. He wanted to take the little blond right there against a tree in the woods, and to hell with everything else.

Keeton stepped back and shook his head. "I think I'll go find Braxton. I won't pretend I'm not attracted to you, Logan, but I won't do this. I know everyone thinks I'm a slut, and maybe I am, but I won't get involved with you while you're with someone else. If you ever find yourself unattached, come find me."

Then he turned and walked away.

Chapter Two

Keeton curled up on the sofa to watch Talon and Boston play pool. After everyone had left, he'd thrown himself into helping clean up the aftermath of Xander's birthday bash. He worked hard so he didn't have to think. Thinking hurt.

"Hey, Blondie, wanna play?"

Keeton looked over at Talon and smiled. "You know I suck, T."

Talon returned his smile and sniggered. "Yeah, I know. Why do you think I want to play you? Tired of getting my ass kicked."

Keeton rolled his eyes. "I'm good. You'll just have to find another way to inflate that already enormous ego."

"Why I never!" Talon slapped his hand to his chest, feigning indignation.

"Drama queen." Keeton snorted as he watched Boston struggling to contain his laughter, his body shaking with the effort.

"So, what did you think of Logan?"

Talon's question caught him off guard. "Well, he seemed nice, I guess. I mean, I only talked to him for a minute." Keeton shrugged. He really didn't want to talk about Logan.

He'd spent the whole afternoon trying not to think about the man. In the end, he gave up—too much work. He couldn't put a finger on it, but something about Logan drew him in like ants to a picnic. Keeton had never seen a more gorgeous man, but that wasn't the reason for his infatuation. He felt it almost as a need. The same as breathing, he *needed* to be close to Logan.

It made no sense, and left him confused and anxious.

Logan had a dazzling aura, though. The core glowed, the same ice blue as his eyes, and all the rings surrounding it flickered in varying shades of blue. It shimmered like all shifter auras did, but Logan's aura also sparked like tiny explosions...or a lightning storm. Keeton had never seen anything like it, and he didn't know what it meant.

He sighed inwardly. It didn't matter. As much as he wanted the man, Logan had a girlfriend. Why did he always seem to attract the taken ones? He never had a shortage of men willing to have a little fun, but none of them stayed longer than the time it took to get off.

Keeton wanted forever. Maybe he was a little outlandish, a little too flamboyant for some, but he just couldn't help it. He'd tried to tune it down for a while a few years back, but it had been wicked boring.

He stood and stretched. He needed a distraction. He should have been working on the character panels for Braxton's new graphic novel, *Quest,* but he just didn't feel it.

"Did you meet Mariah?" Talon smirked.

"Uh..." Hell, he *really* didn't want to talk about her. "Yeah. She seemed nice. Really pretty."

Talon studied him for a minute, then smiled devilishly. "Right. Try again."

Keeton rolled his eyes. "I think your brother is hot as hell, and she's one lucky bitch. I hope they're very happy together," he grumbled. "So happy she chokes on it," he added under his breath.

Boston burst out laughing. Talon looked to be having a hard time not following suit. Keeton just glared at them both and stomped from the room, the effect lost when he tripped over the corner of the area rug and landed face-first at Talon's feet.

Talon lost it, laughing so hard, he doubled over. If Keeton had not been so upset, he would have been amazed. He never saw the gruff brother laugh like that.

Keeton was pissed off and embarrassed, though. He didn't know how much Talon knew, but he realized the man baited him. *Asshole.*

He picked himself up from the floor with as much dignity as he could muster and left the room without another word.

* * * *

"That was a wonderful play, don't you think? Especially for community theater," Mariah chirped from the passenger's seat of Logan's Jeep.

"Mmm hmm." Logan didn't even know what the play had been about. He had spent the entire evening thinking about Keeton and counting the minutes until he could be with him again. He felt a twinge of guilt as he glanced over at Mariah.

He liked the girl, even if she did continue to make him feel uneasy. Logan had caught her staring at him with a slight smirk on her face several times during the play. He didn't know why, but it gnawed at his nerves.

The fact that he didn't feel...anything made him feel like an ass. He didn't want to hurt her, but he had never felt a connection with her.

Not like with his *sienota*—his soul mate, his missing piece. For a few minutes, just for that little space in time when he'd been with Keeton, Logan had felt complete for the first time in his life.

"What's going on, Logan? I can tell something's bothering you. Please, talk to me." Mariah twisted her hands nervously in her lap.

Logan sighed inwardly. He saw no point in dragging out the inevitable. "Yeah, we need to talk. Let's wait until we get to your place, though, okay?"

"You're breaking up with me, aren't you?" She spoke quietly, her voice strained. "It's that little blond, Braxton's friend. I saw it in your eyes today. The way you looked at him." Her breath hitched, but she didn't cry.

"Yes and no. It's more complicated than that. Let's just get you home, and I promise I will explain everything." Well, as much as he could. He never revealed himself to a lover, and the girl sitting in the passenger seat would not change that. Yeah, he liked her, but he didn't know her well enough to trust her with his secrets.

Besides, they weren't just his secrets, and he would do anything to protect his brothers.

"Okay," she said quietly. "Can we swing by your place first? I think I left my cell phone there this afternoon. I can't find it anywhere."

"Sure." He tried to smile at her, but it felt cheap and fake, and he gave it up quickly.

Twenty minutes later, Logan sat on the suede sofa in the living room while Mariah searched for her cell phone. Maybe he could just talk to her here and then have one of his brothers drive her home.

No. He wouldn't take the coward's way out, but that didn't mean he looked forward to it.

And where had everyone gone? Talon and Boston would be at work at the bar, but the rest of the pack should be there, including his mate.

"Found it." Mariah held up her cell phone as she glided into the room. She stopped a few feet from the sofa and looked at him uncertainly. "Why?"

Logan closed his eyes. So, they were going to do this now. Looking up, he gave her a little smile and patted the cushion next to him. "Come here."

Mariah hesitated for just a moment, then slowly moved to sit beside him. "Is it something I did? Something I didn't do?"

"No, honey." Logan turned to face her, taking both of her hands in his. "It's nothing you did or didn't do. You are an amazing woman. Anyone would be lucky to have you." He paused to take a deep breath before continuing. "There's just no…spark, no connection that tells me this is going to become something more permanent. I'm sure you can feel it as well."

She sat for a long time, just looking at him. Finally, she shook her head and squeezed his hands in hers. "No, Logan. You're wrong. I do feel a connection. I love you."

Logan blinked at her and almost groaned. *Ah, shit.* In all the ways he had played the conversation out in his head, he never saw this coming.

"Mariah, we've only known each other for a few weeks. How can you possibly love me? I'm sure you care about me, but love?" He reached up to tuck her hair behind her ear. "You don't love me, sweetheart."

"Yes, I do. I know my own heart, Logan. It's okay that you don't love me back. Not yet. But, I think you will. I can make you so happy. Just give us a little more time." She started crying, and Logan felt more helpless with each passing minute.

* * * *

Keeton stood paralyzed just inside the kitchen doorway. He clutched the bag of marshmallows to his chest and bit his lip. He hadn't meant to eavesdrop. He didn't even realize Logan had returned until he heard his voice in the living room.

Edging a little closer, but keeping to the shadows of the kitchen, he listened to Mariah crying and begging Logan to give them just a little more time. His heart broke for her.

"Mariah, this just isn't working for me. I'm sorry. I do care about you, and I hope we can remain friends, but I don't love you. Not the way you deserve to be loved. This is for the best." Logan spoke so quietly, Keeton had to strain to hear him.

"It's Braxton's friend, isn't it? Keeton?" Her voice hardened.

"Yes and no." Logan sighed, and Keeton could see the tension in his neck and shoulders. Then Logan's words sank in, and Keeton's breath caught in his chest.

He didn't know what to feel. Part of him wanted to dance for joy that Logan wanted to be with him. Another part of him felt like a colossal jerk for the heartache this caused Mariah. Confusion won out, however. He'd only met Logan for a few minutes, but the man seemed willing to throw away what he had with Mariah to be with him.

Keeton frowned. What did Logan mean by "yes and no"? Strangely, he wanted to know more about the "no" part. He had to admit, he would feel a lot better knowing he didn't cause the breakup he witnessed.

"Yes, I feel something for Keeton." Logan shook his head slowly. "I can't explain it." He looked Mariah in the eyes again as he continued. "But, he's not the reason that I don't love you. I'm sorry if that sounds harsh, but I want you to understand. I don't love you, Mariah. And I never will. There's just something missing. I'm so sorry."

Keeton decided to retreat to the campfire. He didn't need to hear any more, and he felt like a prick for not leaving sooner. He took one last look at the couple on the sofa and froze.

Mariah's aura pulsed and swirled, the outer rings bright, vibrant reds and oranges. Where the core should have been, however, there was nothingness—just a huge dark void.

Keeton's stomach rolled. He had to get Logan away from her. He had no idea what it meant, but it could be nothing good. He felt cold. He didn't know how he could see other people's auras, he just did. He had always had the gift, since as long as he could remember. It took a long time to sort out what the different rings and colors meant, but a person's aura always served him well in judging their character.

"Logan," Mariah began in a deceptively sweet tone. Keeton wanted to pull her hair out. "I didn't want you to find out this way, but..." She trailed off, looking down at her knees.

"What is it, honey? Just tell me." Logan placed a finger under her chin and tilted her face up.

She leaned forward, looking over Logan's shoulder, and smiled right at Keeton. He saw the wicked gleam in her eyes before she pressed her lips to Logan's ear and whispered just loud enough for Keeton to hear.

"I'm pregnant. I'm carrying your child."

Chapter Three

Logan jerked back and glared at the woman in front of him. "No."

"Yes," she replied simply. "Will you abandon your child, Logan?"

Logan stood and started pacing in front of the sofa. Of course, he wouldn't abandon his child. If a child existed, which he doubted. He had always been so careful, always worn a condom. He couldn't receive or pass on diseases, but he had never wanted children. He never wanted to take the chance that he would pass on his curse to a child.

"Remember that first night in Atlanta last month? We went to the casinos. You had a lot to drink, and you were all revved up from the money you were winning. We were going back to our room and—"

"We had sex in the elevator." Logan gasped. He stopped pacing, closed his eyes, and let his face fall into his hands.

No, no, fuck no! What the hell was he going to do? He had just found his mate. He hadn't even had time to tell Keeton that he *was* his mate, and now he had to choose. Logan didn't know if he could live without Keeton, without part of his soul, but neither could he walk away from his child. He seriously doubted Mariah would be open to letting him have Keeton and the baby.

She stood and took one of Logan's hands, placing it on her flat stomach. "Our baby," she whispered.

Logan's entire body shook. He felt like he might vomit. He made this mess, and now he would just have to deal with it. Not telling Keeton suddenly didn't seem so bad. Somehow, if he didn't speak it out loud, maybe it wouldn't be true. He would do the right thing, step up and take responsibility for his offspring. He would find a way to live without his *sienota*.

Opening his eyes, he looked at the mother of his child. His heart pounded as he opened his mouth to tell her that he was hers. That he would walk beside her always.

"She's lying, Logan."

Logan jerked his hand away from Mariah's stomach and took a step back, whirling around to see Keeton emerge from the shadows of the kitchen. His mouth watered, and his palms went sweaty as he took in the sight of his mate, his miracle, his angel. Keeton wore a pair of gray sweatpants, riding low on his hips, and a plain black tank top that came down just below his belly button, showing off several inches of creamy skin.

"She's lying, Logan," Keeton repeated.

Logan's brows drew together as he looked between Keeton and Mariah before finally settling his gaze on Keeton. "How do you know?"

"I just do. I'll explain it later," he said with a pointed look at Mariah. "Right now, I just need you to trust me." His eyes turned back to Logan, pleading.

Logan walked to his mate and reached out to gently cup his face. "I have to be sure, angel. This is my child we're talking about."

Keeton nuzzled into Logan's palm for just a moment before he took a step back and shook his head. "There is no child. Please, trust me."

God, Logan wanted to believe him, wanted to trust him, but he needed proof. He needed to know what Keeton knew, what made him so positive Mariah deceived him.

Keeton cast an icy glare at Mariah and growled, "Tell him the truth."

Tears streamed down her cheeks. "I swear it's the truth. I'm pregnant."

"Liar!" Keeton spat.

Logan didn't know what to do. Thankfully, Braxton, Xander, and

Jackson chose that moment to walk in through the kitchen door, laughing and talking loudly. They all froze and fell silent, taking in the scene in the living room.

"What's going on?" Jackson asked hesitantly.

"She," Keeton pointed at Mariah, "is a lying skank." His eyes never left Mariah, and he stared at her for several seconds before his calm façade collapsed. "Tell him the fucking truth!" he yelled, spittle flying from his mouth.

Braxton rushed over to Keeton and threw his arms around him. Logan had to bite back the urge to growl and snatch his mate away from the little man. "What's going on, Kee?"

Mariah answered, "I'm pregnant. It's Logan's."

Everyone went quiet again, except Keeton. "You are not pregnant, you vile, selfish, manipulating whore!"

Mariah stepped up to Keeton and gave him a watery smile. "I know you're attracted to him. He is gorgeous. I also know you're hurting, but you have to accept this."

Keeton stepped toward her until they stood toe-to-toe. "Why are you doing this to him?" His voice came low and dangerous, cold as ice.

Mariah leaned closer and whispered something in Keeton's ear Logan couldn't hear. He saw Keeton's body tense, his face turning a brilliant shade of red, and he exploded. "He does not fucking belong to you!"

Braxton moved to stand in front of Keeton, insinuating himself between his best friend and Mariah. "I believe you, Kee. I believe you."

* * * *

"Tell us what you know," Braxton murmured.

Keeton took a deep breath and shut his eyes, squeezing them tight. He couldn't look at Logan, didn't want to see the look of disbelief or contempt on his face. "When my mom was pregnant with my little sister, Anna, there was always a small white glow in the core of her aura. All pregnant women have it. I've never seen one that didn't. Even if they're horrible women, they have that little white glow. Babies are just so pure and innocent, ya know."

"And Mariah doesn't have this glow?" Xander spoke for the first time since he had walked into the room.

Keeton relaxed a little. Xander knew he could see auras, and the big alpha sounded like he believed him.

"No, she doesn't." Keeton hesitated to tell them that the woman's aura held no core at all. He always associated the nucleus of someone's aura with the purity of their soul. The fact that the crazy bitch's aura had no center scared the shit out of him. Did that mean she had no soul? How was that even possible?

Mariah snorted derisively, and everyone turned to look at her. "You aren't buying this crap, are you?" She sneered at Keeton. "This is ridiculous. Auras?" She turned to look at Logan. "Baby?"

Keeton finally allowed himself to look at Logan as well, unsurprised to find the man staring back. The look of hope and helplessness vying for dominance on Logan's face broke his heart. Keeton took a step toward him and held out his hand. "I swear to you, I'm telling the truth."

"Logan?" Mariah's smugness started to fade. She sounded uncertain for the first time since the conversation began. Keeton didn't even glance at her, nor did Logan.

"I want to believe you." Logan took Keeton's outstretched hand in both of his. "I mean, I do believe you about seeing auras, but what if you're wrong this time? Haven't you ever made a mistake before?"

"Oh for fuck's sake, Logan!" Braxton yelled, causing everyone to jump. "Are you a paramedic or not? Draw some damn blood, or make her pee in a cup, and take it to the hospital. Hell, I'll go out and buy a home pregnancy test. Talk about ridiculous."

Everyone stared at Braxton in shock. "What?" he snapped.

Xander wrapped his arms around him and nuzzled his face into Braxton's neck. "I love you, *chulo*," he said around a chuckle.

Logan stared at the floor, frowning. "Why the hell didn't I think of that?" He turned to Mariah. "Your call. Blood or urine?"

Keeton took great pleasure in watching the color drain from the woman's face. Her eyes went wide, and she took a step back. "You believe him?" she asked in a thin voice.

"If you are carrying my child, I don't see what the problem is. We can get this all sorted out right now." Logan sounded deceptively calm, but Keeton could see the muscles in his jaw twitch, and his hands repeatedly fisted and relaxed.

Gotcha, bitch. He probably could have stopped the grin that spread over his face, but he didn't.

"But it's too soon for it to show up on a test," she sputtered.

"Then how do you know you're pregnant?" Jackson asked.

"A woman just knows these things," she snapped at him.

"Not good enough. So, what's it going to be?" Logan asked again.

The room fell silent for several minutes. Finally, Mariah clenched her fists at her sides and glared daggers at Keeton. "You'll be sorry for this. I'm not someone you want as an enemy. Just ask my legion."

Keeton's head shot up when he heard Logan's deep growl. It sounded feline and feral, and did amazing things to his insides.

Mariah marched across the room, glaring over her shoulder at Keeton one last time. Then she stomped out the door, slamming it behind her.

Logan spun around and swept Keeton into his arms, crushing him to the hard, muscled wall of his chest. Logan's lips brushed over his temple, causing him to shiver as his heart threatened to beat through his sternum.

Then, without warning, Logan lifted him into the air. Keeton scrambled to hold on, locking his legs around Logan's waist and clutching at his broad shoulders. One big hand cupped his ass, holding him up. The other wrapped around the back of his neck and pulled him close.

"Thank you," Logan whispered against his lips. He crushed his mouth down on Keeton's, sucking and nibbling. Keeton gasped in surprise, and Logan took full advantage, pushing his tongue into his mouth and devouring him.

Keeton swept his tongue against Logan's, happy to let the bigger man take control and lead him. He wiggled and whimpered, trying his best to get even closer. He'd crawl inside the guy's skin if he could. Logan felt so warm, smelled so good, and he kissed like a dream.

"Slut." Braxton's voice brought Keeton crashing back to reality. He broke the kiss and buried his face in Logan's neck, his cheeks flaming. What the hell was wrong with him? He had never been embarrassed like this before. Then again, he usually made the first move. He never had a man completely consume him as Logan had just done.

"Get a room," Braxton said with a smirk in his voice.

Keeton groaned and pushed his face tighter to Logan's heated flesh. He felt the rumble in Logan's chest as he laughed along with Braxton.

"So, are you going to tell him?" Xander asked suddenly.

Logan's laughter stopped immediately. Keeton raised his head and glanced at Xander then back at Logan. "Tell me what?" He watched as the big man in his arms glared at his best friend's lover. "Logan?"

Xander just smiled a shit-eating grin, then wrapped his arms around Braxton again, pulling him close to his big body.

Keeton looked from Xander and Braxton, to Logan, then back, several times. His eyes widened, and his heart pounded as realization dawned on him. *Oh, shit!* He stopped breathing and his stomach did a backflip as he gazed at Logan, staring into the eyes of his mate.

Chapter Four

"Keeton!" Braxton yelled as he paced Keeton's living room. "Are you even listening to me?"

Keeton glared at his best friend. "Yeah. It's kind of hard not to when you're screaming like a banshee."

Braxton returned his glare and flopped down heavily on the love seat. "You are being a filthy hypocrite," he grumbled.

Keaton rolled his eyes, but remained silent. What could he say? He knew Braxton was right. Not that he would admit it, but still, he knew.

"What was it you told me when I came over here, freaking out about being mated to Xander?" Braxton leaned forward, and his tone softened. "Keeton, why don't you want to be mated to Logan? I thought you'd be happy."

Keeton sighed. "Do you even understand what this means? If I am Logan's mate, then that means I have shifter blood in me as well."

"Believe me, I know." Braxton snorted, shaking his head.

Keeton had to smile. He remembered very well trying to calm his friend when Braxton learned not only had he mated a shifter, but that he was part furry beastie as well.

Shifters only ever mated with other shifters. Even though both Keeton and Braxton couldn't shift, they apparently did have some diluted shifter blood.

"Keeton, you are such an idiot sometimes." Braxton held up his hand to forestall Keeton's retort. "Honey, your grandmother is a shifter, yes?"

Keeton nodded.

"Then that means that your dad does have some shifter blood. It is just too diluted for him to shift. Therefore, you have some shifter genes as well."

"I know." Keeton sighed again. "I just never thought about it before now."

"Well, what's the problem?"

Keeton didn't know how to explain. Though he had always wanted forever with someone, he had doubts that he could measure up to *forever* material. He easily became bored, started fights for no reason, pushed the limits, and tested the boundaries. He was often stubborn and impulsive, always easily distracted, and he could be sensitive to a fault.

Simply put, he was an utter mess.

His grandmother, uncle, and cousin were shifters, so he knew a little about the culture. If Keeton mated with Logan, it was a lifetime gig. No option of divorce, no separation, no "It didn't work out, but have a nice life." Keeton would always be bound to Logan, and Logan to him.

"What if he doesn't like me?" he whispered. Logan would never have another true mate, and forever seemed one hell of a commitment.

"You won't know unless you give him a chance." Braxton climbed to his feet, leaned over, and kissed the top of Keeton's head. "Just think about it, okay? I have to get going before Xander wets himself wondering where I am." He rolled his eyes as he straightened and headed for the door. "Overprotective idiot," he grumbled under his breath.

"Thanks, Brax. I just need some time. I'll call you."

After Braxton left, Keeton stretched out on the couch and stared at the ceiling. What would it be like to have someone worry about him? Someone that wanted to take care of him, make sure he was safe, comfortable, and happy. What would it be like to have someone like Logan Cartwright to love him?

* * * *

Logan sat on the edge of his bed, staring down at his feet. It had been almost a week, and he still hadn't seen or heard from Keeton.

He rubbed at his chest over his heart. He could feel the steady beat beneath his palm, but that couldn't be right. His heart was broken, ripped from his chest, and walked on. No way should it still be functioning.

"Fuck," he muttered as he pushed to his feet. He could still see the look of shock on Keeton's face. He had known the exact moment that Keeton pieced it together. His little body had tensed in Logan's arms, his eyes as big around as saucers, and his heart rate had accelerated, beating frantically against Logan's chest.

Then with one simple little word, breathed so quietly he almost hadn't heard it, Keeton had shattered Logan's entire world.

"No."

That's all Keeton had said. Logan didn't remember much after that. He vaguely recalled easing Keeton to his feet and climbing the stairs to his room. Then Talon came, almost beating down his door, shouting at him to get his sorry ass up and go to work. That had been four days ago. He didn't even know how long he'd been in his room before that.

Just give him time. Braxton had been constantly telling him that all week. Sometimes Logan just wanted to punch the little shit in the ear.

He looked around the room, forgot what he'd been about to do, shrugged, and climbed back into bed. He pulled a pillow to him, curling around it, and closed his eyes. A knock on the door had him groaning into the sheets.

"Go away."

The doorknob jiggled, and Logan mentally patted himself on the back for remembering to lock the door.

"Logan Edward Cartwright, open this fucking door, or I swear I'll have Xander break it down!" Braxton shouted through the wood.

Logan groaned again and rolled from the bed. Braxton didn't make empty threats. He would have Xander break down the damn door, and Xander would do it. He'd do anything for his mate. Even destroy the house.

"What the hell do you want?" Logan yelled, pulling the door open and letting it bang against the wall. Xander wasn't the only one that could fuck up the house. He didn't even look at Braxton, but went and climbed back in his bed.

"Edward?" a curious voice asked from the doorway. "Seriously?"

Logan sprang up from the bed so quickly, his head spun. He stumbled halfway to the door before his legs gave out, and he folded to his knees. He knelt there on the floor, staring openly at the most beautiful sight he'd ever seen.

"You drunk?"

Logan just shook his head mutely.

Keeton wrinkled his nose as he stepped inside the room. "It smells like a bag of assholes in here." Then he leaned in, and sniffed at Logan. "Sweet hell! When's the last time you showered?"

Logan couldn't remember, didn't really care. He just continued to drink in the sight of the angel in front of him.

Keeton stared back at him for a minute before he rolled his eyes and snorted. "Okay, shower, food, and *then* we will talk." He reached out to help Logan to his feet, and pushed him toward the door. "I'll try and clean up this toxic waste site you call a bedroom."

Logan looked over his shoulder as he stepped out into the hall. He didn't want to leave—didn't want to let Keeton out of his sight. He opened his mouth, but Keeton waved a hand, cutting him off.

The smile Keeton gave him was so sweet it made his knees weak. "I'll be here."

Logan nodded once and hurried down the hall to the bathroom.

* * * *

Keeton began picking up the dirty clothes strewn across Logan's room. They were everywhere—on the floor, the bed, the dresser, even draped over the lamps. He deposited them all in the empty hamper, then grabbed the trashcan from behind the door and started collecting the empty beer bottles. There were dozens of them on the nightstands, the dresser, and he even found a few under the bed. Next, he removed the sheets and blankets from Logan's bed and tossed them in the hamper as well. He found new linens in the closet and quickly remade the bed.

When he finally finished, Keeton sat down on the edge of the bed and sighed. He hadn't believed Braxton when he told him how depressed Logan was.

He, himself, had been miserable all week. Hell, his room probably looked worse than Logan's. He couldn't sleep, and he had barely eaten since leaving after Xander's birthday party. The only things that came easily were thoughts of Logan.

Logan appeared in the doorway just as Keeton stood to pull back the curtains.

He nearly swallowed his tongue. Logan wore only a towel, slung low on his hips. Water dripped from the ends of his hair, and he watched Keeton uncertainly.

Keeton felt his heart stutter at the guarded expression in the man's eyes. He knew Logan had good reason to regard him in such a way. He wanted to do something, say anything, to reassure him, but he was just as nervous as his…mate.

I might as well get used to saying it.

His longest relationship had lasted exactly twenty-four days. What the hell did he know about being someone's mate or partner? He had already been freaking out about the whole Mariah-doesn't-have-a-soul thing, and then they had dropped the big M-bomb in his lap.

He also understood about the compulsion shifters had to be near their mates. Maybe Logan only wanted him because of the connection. Keeton would not be content with being only a consolation prize. He wanted the blue ribbon. He needed someone to love him, not just be stuck with him.

He looked back to Logan, surprised to find him still standing in the doorway, staring down at his feet and looking completely dejected.

"Morton Salt," Keeton said.

Logan looked at him blankly.

"You know, 'When it rains, it pours.'" He snorted when Logan continued to look at him in confusion.

"Never mind." He walked across the room to Logan and stopped right in front of him. "I'm sorry. I panicked, and I handled it badly. I can't promise you anything, but I'm willing to try."

Keeton took the last step, pressed his body against Logan's, and wrapped his arms lightly around his narrow waist. "I don't know anything about you, but I want to. I feel the connection, and I know it's probably just a stupid shifter pheromone thing, but I was miserable this week," he whispered. "So, can we just take it slow?"

Logan just nodded. Keeton frowned when he realized that Logan hadn't spoken a word since Keeton arrived in the room. Though Keeton still had his arms wrapped around him, the big man's arms hung limply at his sides.

He quickly released his hold and took an unsteady step back. Maybe Logan had changed his mind.

He gave a very unmanly squeak when Logan's arms roped around him without warning and crushed Keeton so tightly to his broad chest that it squeezed the air from his lungs.

"We can go as slow as you want, angel. Take all the time you need, just please don't leave me again," Logan murmured into his hair.

Keeton struggled until Logan's arms loosened around him, and he could push back to look up into those beautiful ice blue eyes. "I can't promise I won't leave, but I do promise to give this a chance."

He expected Logan to be hurt or angry with him, but he just smiled. "Okay. I can live with that." He kissed Keeton's temple, his forehead, his nose, and finally his lips, just a sweet, chaste brush against his mouth. "I'm going to make you so happy that you will never want to leave."

Keeton let his head fall back as Logan trailed kisses along his throat and across his shoulders. "No biting," he warned breathlessly. "No claiming allowed."

Logan stilled for a second before he went back to licking and nibbling along Keeton's collarbones. "Can I mark you? Have my scent on you?"

A moan escaped Keeton's parted lips, and he arched his body against his soon-to-be lover's. "Yes." He tugged on the towel around Logan's waist until it fell to the floor.

Slowly, he moved his hands across Logan's hips and down the man's massive thighs. He finally reached Logan's thick cock, taking it in one hand and using the other to cup his heavy sac. Wow…Logan was big. Keeton had to see it.

He leaned away from Logan's searching mouth to try to get a more direct view of the monster in his hand. He gulped audibly when Logan finally stood to give him unobstructed access to his gorgeous body.

His dick was huge! Long and thick, cut, and lined with pulsing veins. The head leaked freely from the slit, engorged and dark red, a perfect mushroom shape, and the size of a fucking golf ball. "It won't fit," Keeton muttered, shaking his head slowly.

Chapter Five

Logan chuckled at the astonished look on his mate's face. "Of course it will. You were made for me, baby."

Keeton shook his head. "That thing was made for hitting touchdowns or slaying dragons. It was not made to fit in my ass."

Logan laughed louder. *Hitting touchdowns?* Keeton was adorable.

So what if every fiber of his being cried out for him to claim his mate? Keeton wasn't ready, but he said Logan could mark him. He fully intended to do just that. He planned to bathe Keeton in his scent so everyone would know that he belonged to Logan. He would do everything in his power to prove to Keeton just how much he needed him, how much he loved him. Oh yes, he loved his mate.

He had never believed in love at first sight. Things like that only happened in fairy tales and bedtime stories. One look at the angel before him, one taste of his sweet skin, had converted him. Just like that, Logan was a believer.

Keeton probably wouldn't believe him, not yet, but Logan knew how to be patient.

The beast in him raged and gnashed its teeth, begging him to dominate the smaller man. Demanding Logan claim Keeton and make him submit.

He caged the beast and tried to calm himself. He promised to take things slowly.

A soft moan brought Logan out of his thoughts and back to the moment. He wrapped a choke leash around his own desires and returned his focus to Keeton. He watched as his mate slowly licked his lips, still staring down at Logan's cock.

Biting back a groan, Logan shook, his body vibrating with his effort to hold himself in check. He was already hard enough to pound railroad spikes, and Keeton had barely even touched him. Hell, he hadn't even seen his little man naked yet.

"Clothes off." The order spilled from his mouth before he even registered a conscious thought to say it.

Keeton's head snapped up, and his eyes locked with Logan's. He held his breath, hoping against hope that he wasn't about to be told off. Then Keeton's eyes widened, his face flushed, and his breathing sped.

Interesting.

Keeton danced backward and slowly pulled his T-shirt over his head, tossing it at Logan. He put a little extra sway in his hips, rubbing his hands over every inch of creamy skin he revealed. His hands glided up his bare chest and pinched both nipples, tweaking, twisting, and pulling at them. His head fell back, and he moaned, still swinging his hips to some nonexistent beat.

Logan reached down and gripped the base of his cock to keep from coming right then and there. He had never seen anything so erotic, so arousing, so completely drool worthy in his life.

He groaned as the strip show continued. Keeton even made the act of kicking off his flip-flops look sexy as hell. He flipped open the top button of his jeans, slid down the zipper, and shimmied and gyrated until the fabric fell to pool around his ankles.

Logan hadn't missed the fact that underwear was missing from the pile of clothing Keeton had just removed. He was also very aware that his mate appeared completely smooth, no hair any place that Logan could see. He gripped his dick harder and took a deep breath, trying to calm his racing libido.

Bad idea. The scent of his mate combined with the scent of his mate's arousal left him panting. Add to that the way Keeton still undulated in the middle of the room and Logan didn't think he'd ever breathe right again.

"On your knees, hands behind your back, and no touching." Logan spoke roughly, his voice deep and commanding. He had to swallow back his whoop of victory when Keeton immediately knelt in front of him and linked his fingers behind his back.

The look in Keeton's eyes as he gazed up at Logan was one of total trust—and a whole lot of lust. Logan wanted this bad—his leaking cock agreed wholeheartedly—but he had to be sure.

"What do you want, baby?"

Never looking away from Logan's eyes, Keeton licked his lips again. "I want to suck your cock, sir."

Logan groaned again as his eyes rolled back in his head. He knew that his *sienota* was his other half, the yin to his yang, the missing piece to the whole. He never expected Keeton to be so perfect for him, though. *Thank you, fate!*

Everything about him, from the tip of his blond, gelled spikes, to the bottom of his tiny, elegant feet, made Logan ache and want. He needed to be the dominant partner. He didn't know if it came from his DNA, or just part of his psyche, but he needed to control his mate. Keeton appeared more than willing to submit to Logan. He even seemed to be getting off on it.

Logan reached down to stroke his lover's soft cheek for just a moment, then stood straight, letting his hands drop to his sides. He didn't say a word, just nodded at him.

Keeton smiled, then swooped in to envelop the head of Logan's cock into his hot, wet mouth.

Oh, sweet mercy! He'd been too hard for too long, and his body screamed for release. He bit his lip, closed his eyes, and tried to think of anything besides his mate's lips wrapped around his aching cock.

He failed miserably when Keeton pulled back, teasing Logan's slit with his tongue, then dived back down until the engorged head of Logan's prick hit the back of his sweet little throat. Not many lovers—men or women—had been able to take all of him. Logan had to see it.

He opened his eyes and looked down just as Keeton swallowed, contracting the muscles in his throat and squeezing Logan's prick. "Oh, fuck," Logan groaned. The sight of his glistening shaft, sliding in and out of full, pink lips stretched taut over his hard flesh, had his balls drawing up close to his body.

He tangled both hands in Keeton's hair and gave a sharp tug. "Enough."

Keeton let Logan's cock slip from his mouth and sat back on his heels, giving him a curious look. "What? Did I do something wrong?"

"Oh, no, angel. I just don't want to come yet. Not until I have this dragon slayer buried deep inside that pretty ass of yours." Logan swallowed hard at the raw desire shining from his lover's eyes. "Get on the bed, on your hands and knees, and no touching yourself."

He had to bite the inside of his cheek to keep from chuckling when Keeton sprang up from the floor and practically dove onto the bed in his eagerness to comply. Logan moved around to the side of the bed, pulling a bottle of lube from the nightstand. He crawled up on the mattress, positioning himself behind Keeton, nudging his legs wider.

Placing a small kiss between Keeton's shoulder blades he whispered, "I can't give or receive human diseases, so we don't need the condoms."

Keeton peeked over his shoulder and smiled. "Yes, I know."

Logan returned the smile before pushing gently on the back of Keeton's head. Keeton eased his head and chest down to the mattress, his ass still high in the air. "No coming until I say, Keeton. Do you understand?"

When he received no reply, Logan gave a light slap to Keeton's ass. "I expect to be answered when I ask you a question. Now, do you understand?"

Keeton moaned before gasping out, "Yes, sir."

Damn, Logan could get used to hearing that.

* * * *

If Logan didn't get that big, gorgeous cock in his ass in the next three seconds, Keeton was going to lose his damn mind. He couldn't believe Logan's dominance had him so cranked up. Keeton hated people ordering him around, in or out of the bedroom. He was just too stubborn, too independent, too high-spirited to allow anyone to tame him.

Yet, there he knelt, ass in the air, hands fisted in the sheets, and panting like a bitch in heat. His dick ached and throbbed, the tip weeping copiously. Raising himself just enough to look down his body, he watched the rock-hard flesh swinging freely between his legs, jerking with each beat of his heart.

Another smack to his ass, harder than before, had him moaning long and low as he eased his chest back to the sheets.

"Don't move." Logan's commanding tone sent electricity racing up and down his spine. The need to submit to his lover, to please him, overwhelmed Keeton, and he shuddered.

Logan's hands moved over the rounded hills of his upturned ass, slowly, torturously, rubbing and squeezing. Keeton felt cool air breeze across his quivering opening when Logan gently parted his cheeks.

"Damn, baby." The click of a bottle cap, a pause, and then a slick finger caressed him, slowly ringing his entrance. "Mm, so pretty." The thick, lusty quality of Logan's voice washed over Keeton, dragging a ragged moan from his lips.

The stroking finger pushed in, breaching the outer ring of muscles, and Keeton gasped. Damn, it felt good, and he wanted more. He couldn't remember ever being this hard. As if sensing his need, Logan pulled out and two fingers pushed back in. Keeton pushed against Logan's fingers, forgetting his order to not move, wiggling his ass and silently begging for more.

"That's it, baby. Fuck yourself. This tight little ass is going to look so nice wrapped around my cock." Logan pushed in a third finger, raking over Keeton's sweet spot.

His head came up off the bed, and he cried out, desperately willing himself not to come. "Logan! Please, I need you. Fuck me!"

"Shh, baby, I need to stretch you more. I don't want to hurt you. One more finger." Logan pulled out then pushed back in with four fingers.

Keeton moaned loudly, his body shaking with the effort to hold back his orgasm. It burned a little, but not nearly enough for him to want to stop. "Logan!"

"Okay, angel, okay. Relax." A strong hand stroked down Keeton's spine, and Logan's fingers disappeared, replaced by the bulbous head of his cock. He slipped the crown past the guarding ring of muscles, and slowly, so slowly, pushed forward.

"Oh fucking hell," Logan groaned. "Damn, you're tight. So, hot. Like a fucking inferno."

Keeton echoed his lover's groan. *Fucking hell* was right. He thought it might have less to do with his tight ass, and more that Logan's cock was ginormous! He had told Logan it wouldn't fit. By the time he finished feeding his cock to Keeton's ass, he would probably puncture a kidney.

Just when he knew that he couldn't take any more, he felt Logan's hips brush against his ass, and his lover stilled.

Oh, God, it burned. Keeton bit his lip to keep from crying out. His erection began to wilt, and his muscles contracted, trying to force out the invading monster lodged in his ass. Logan groaned, his hands clutching at Keeton's hips.

"Ready?"

"Yes." *No.* "Move."

Logan pulled back, then pushed in, again and again, slow and steady. The burn began to ease as Keeton relaxed, and his muscles stretched and loosened further. Logan's cock grazed over his prostate with every thrust, sending him into a tailspin of pleasure and desire.

Keeton moaned and writhed as his flagging erection sprang back to life, throbbing and pulsing, leaking pre-cum against his belly. He couldn't believe just moments before he had almost begged Logan to stop. Damn, it felt amazing.

"Let me make you feel good. Tell me what you want, angel." Logan touched every inch of Keeton he could reach. He stroked and soothed, grasped and kneaded, leaving a trail of fire after his roaming hands.

"Harder. Please, Logan. Please…I need…I…oh, shit!" Keeton groaned when Logan leaned forward, changing the angle, and driving even deeper into his clutching channel.

He felt so swamped in sensations, he didn't know where he ended and Logan began. Logan lay over him, blanketing him, nuzzling the back of his neck. Keeton knew he marked him, drowning him in his mate's scent.

"Do you want to come, baby? Is that what you need?"

"Oh, God, please, yes," Keeton whimpered.

Logan sat up, gripped both of Keeton's hips, and began thrusting into him, harder, faster. He pulled back on Keeton's hips with each thrust, pushing in as deep as he could go. "Then come now," Logan ground out. He changed the angle, nailing Keeton's sweet spot again. "Come for me, angel."

Lights exploded behind Keeton's closed eyelids, and his head swam. He cried out, yelling Logan's name, as hot, sticky cum shot from his slit in long, creamy ropes. It covered Keeton's stomach, his chest, and the sheets under him.

Logan groaned, wrapping his arms around Keeton's torso, and pulling his back to Logan's warm, sweaty, chest. He continued to pound into him, drawing out his orgasm, until he sagged in Logan's arms.

"Who do you belong to, Keeton? I want to hear you say it." Logan growled sensuously in his ear.

He couldn't fight it. He had never felt like this with anyone before, and he was sure he never would again. Wherever Logan went, that's where Keeton wanted—needed—to be.

"You, Logan. I belong to you," he whispered. He turned his head and captured his lover's mouth with his own.

Logan whimpered, actually whimpered, and Keeton had never heard a sweeter sound. "Come for me, Logan. Show me I'm yours," he murmured against Logan's lips, before sealing their mouths together once more.

Logan groaned into his mouth as his body froze and tensed. He felt the heat of Logan's orgasm deep within his dark tunnel and gloried in it. This big, strong, beautiful, man wanted him. All he had to do was reach out and take him, accept him, and stop holding back.

Chapter Six

Logan lay on his back, staring up at the ceiling, a contented smile on his face. His mate draped over him, his face nuzzled into his neck, and everything felt right in the world. He hadn't claimed Keeton, but he could smell his scent all over his little mate, and it made him want to purr.

Soon, Keeton would be ready to take that last step. He thought his heart would burst with happiness when Keeton said he belonged to him. He longed to claim his mate, though. He needed that bond. Logan never wanted to live without his *sienota*.

A soft groan against his throat had Logan glancing down at his mate. "What is it, baby? Do you hurt?" Perhaps he had been too rough with his lover. He prayed not.

"I'm such a slut," Keeton grumbled.

Logan bit his tongue to keep from laughing. "Why do you say that?"

"Well, considering that your cum is still leaking out of my ass, I thought the answer would be obvious."

He did chuckle then. He knew they needed to get up and shower, but he liked that his seed filled his mate. More proof that Keeton belonged to him. "Having sex with your mate does not a slut make."

Keeton sat up and looked at him seriously. "Not thirty minutes ago, I was going on about how we should take this slow. The next thing I know, I'm practically begging you to fuck my brains out." He dropped his face into his hands and groaned again.

Very gently, Logan pulled his lover's hands away and tilted his face up. "Stop. You are not a slut. Though if you feel the urge, I promise you can take out your sexual frustrations on me." He winked, eliciting a small laugh from Keeton.

"You are beautiful, charming, sexy, amazing, brilliant, and a whole lot of other adjectives I'll ask Braxton for later." He smiled at the giggles coming from his mate. "But not a slut. You said everyone thinks you are. Exactly how many men have you been with?"

Not a question he normally asked his lovers. Not only was it none of his business, but it didn't really matter. He wanted to know everything about his mate, though, and he needed to get to the bottom of Keeton's self-debasing attitude.

Keeton's cheeks burned red, and he chewed on his lower lip. Logan raised an eyebrow, but otherwise kept mute.

Keeton mumbled something he couldn't hear and tried to look away, but Logan caught his chin, preventing his escape. "What was that, angel?"

"One," Keeton murmured dejectedly.

Logan just sat there with his mouth open, no words coming out. When he could finally form a coherent sentence, he asked, "Why in the hell would you, or anyone else, think you were a slut if you've only been with one man?"

"I've had a lot of boyfriends. Well, I don't know if you'd call them boyfriends exactly, but I've been out on my share of dates. I've jerked and sucked a lot of guys off and vice versa, but only had actual intercourse with one man." Keeton still tried desperately to look anywhere but at Logan.

"That still doesn't answer my question."

Keeton sighed, finally meeting Logan's eyes. "I guess because I'm so...out there...everyone just assumes that I'm this big whore. Hell, even Braxton thinks I've slept with every guy that breathes on me." He rolled his eyes at that before continuing. "It was just easier to let people think what they wanted. Better than being a twenty-six-year-old virgin loser," he mumbled.

Logan had to strain to hear the last part. He ground his teeth together and fought to control his breathing. He couldn't pinpoint exactly why the hell he was so angry, but the shifter in him demanded that he protect his mate—even if it was only his mate's reputation.

Reaching up, he gently palmed Keeton's cheek. "Angel, you are perfect. I wouldn't care if you'd had sex with a hundred men, at the same time. I would still think you were perfect. Though, I have to admit, being only the second man to take you—"

"First," Keeton whispered, cutting Logan off.

He stilled as the blood drained from his face. Flashes of their lovemaking streamed through his mind—him pushing, commanding, and dominating his lover. He had been so rough with his mate.

He closed his eyes and winced. Fuck! He'd even taken Keeton from behind, shoving his face into the mattress like a two-dollar whore.

I was the first.

The thought made Logan's stomach clench painfully. What had he done? He had laughed when Keeton voiced his fears that Logan was too big, completely dismissing his concerns. If Keeton had never had anal sex before, Logan probably felt like a damn two-by-four.

He had only one job, one directive. His main purpose in Keeton's life was to protect and cherish him.

Well, he had fucked that up spectacularly. *Nice job, asshole.*

Rolling away from his mate, he climbed out of bed. Grabbing clothes from his closet, he dressed quickly, never looking at Keeton. Disgust at himself made his insides boil. He wanted to scream, to lash out, hit something, but he held back, not wanting to frighten his lover.

I was the first.

Keeton had come to him, trusted him, giving freely to him, wanting only to take things slowly in return. So, Logan, being the upstanding guy that he was, had seen what he wanted to see, heard what he wanted to hear, and forced himself on his inexperienced mate.

A throbbing ache started in his chest. He thought Keeton wanted to be with him, but perhaps he had misinterpreted the younger man's signals. God, he was so confused, so frustrated with his lack of control. Keeton's first time—their first time together—should have been special. He should have taken his time, explored the gift of Keeton's body.

"Logan?"

He paused at his name, softly spoken by his lover. Turning slowly, he held on to his control by a thread. He would not beg forgiveness from his angel. He didn't deserve it.

I was the first.

"I am so sorry, baby," he whispered.

"What? Why are you sorry?" Keeton held out his arms, and Logan couldn't stop himself from moving into them. He crawled back into bed and pulled his mate to him gently.

"I should have done things differently."

"Logan, I'm not following. What are you talking about?"

Shaking his head, Logan pulled away and stood from the bed again. He needed to think, and he couldn't do it with the scent of their combined seed filling his head. "I'm going to run," he said abruptly. "I just need to think. I'll be back."

"Logan, wait!"

He didn't. He slipped through the door, closing it quietly behind him.

* * * *

Keeton sat on the bed in stunned silence as he watched Logan flee from the room. What the hell had just happened? Why did Logan run from him?

Making love to Logan had been the single most amazing experience of Keeton's life. Sure, he was a little sore, but he expected it. If his reward for a little discomfort came in the form of a sizzling hot, blond shifter, he would not trade a second of it. Logan made him feel cherished, loved, wanted, and needed. Even when Logan had been buried balls deep in his ass, even as he dominated and overwhelmed him, he had felt safe and protected.

So, why had his lover practically sprinted out the door? Why had Logan apologized? A sudden thought occurred to him, and his chest tightened painfully. Maybe Logan had changed his mind. It seemed the bigger man couldn't get away fast enough once Keeton told him he had been his first lover.

He remembered Logan's face right before he'd walked out of the room. He had looked so sad, so despondent, and Keeton thought he detected a hint of anger under all that misery. Not at him, but directed inward. Damn, he was so confused.

"What the hell?" he mumbled under his breath.

"He thinks he hurt you."

Keeton looked up, then checked to make sure the sheet covered him. His best friend walked into the room and climbed up on the bed beside him. "Brax, what the hell just happened here?"

Braxton shook his head. "I don't know, sweetheart, but you need to go talk to him. He's hurting, and he needs you."

"I told him he couldn't claim me," Keeton whispered, looking down at his hands where they rested in his lap.

"Smart."

He snapped his attention back to the man beside him. "What?" He thought Braxton would be upset with him.

"I didn't let Xander claim me right away. You barely even know him. Of course, you shouldn't let him claim you. Once you do, there's no out clause, Kee. It's for life." Braxton took a deep breath before he continued. "I won't lie. He will be devastated if you deny him. If you allow him to take you as his own and *then* deny him, however, it will destroy him."

Keeton said nothing, but his heart ached. He knew shifters mated for life. He was Logan's one shot at true happiness. There would never be another. *No pressure or anything.*

Though he was beginning to suspect the same might be true in reverse. He had spent less than three hours total with Logan since they met, but he already couldn't imagine being without him. The whole week he spent away from the man, he felt a big hole in his chest, like some vital part of his being was missing.

"I'll have to watch everyone I love grow old and die," Keeton whispered. He yelped when Braxton reached out his hand and smacked him in the back of the head.

"Keeton you are the youngest member of your family. Not to be a bitch, but you're going to watch them grow old and die either way. Besides…you'll still have me." Braxton preened, drawing a snort from Keeton. "And you're going to grow old right along with the rest of us. Shifters don't live forever—maybe past their hundredth birthday. It's not really that big of a deal."

Keeton groaned. He really hated it when Braxton went all logical on him. What his friend said made sense, but still…

"What if I can't make him happy?"

"You're his mate. You make him happy by breathing," Xander answered from the doorway.

"And you can't make him any more miserable than he's making himself." Talon trailed in behind Xander.

Keeton had the urge to yell for Boston and Jackson. They could just have one big party.

He pulled the sheet tighter around his waist and frowned when Boston and Jackson filed into the room, taking up ranks beside Xander and Talon. *Let the party begin.*

"What are you so afraid of, Keeton?" Boston asked.

Keeton opened his mouth to respond, but shut it quickly. His brow wrinkled, and he pursed his lips. What *was* he afraid of? A strong, kind, gorgeous man wanted him.

Looking at each of the men in the room, he bit his bottom lip before blurting, "Explain about *sienotas* again."

"As Logan's mate, that means you have some watered-down

shifter blood." Xander began the tutorial on Mating 101.

Keeton nodded. He knew that. They needed to get to the good stuff.

"So, once you exchange blood with Logan, and he claims you, your little furry beastie will be unleashed. You will age as a shifter, you'll never get sick, never be susceptible to disease, and you'll be a hell of a lot less breakable," Braxton rattled off.

"Will I turn into an animal on the full moon?" Keeton didn't know how he felt about that.

"That depends on how pure the shifter blood in you is. Since you do not shift now, it's pretty unlikely," Xander said. "You also know that your life force will be bound to Logan's. If Logan dies, so will you. The same works in reverse."

Keeton swallowed hard. Yeah, he knew that, but he didn't really want to think about anyone dying.

"No one has ever needed me before," Keeton mumbled. Therein lay the crux. Logan needed him, and Keeton knew if he let himself, he could easily fall in love with the big shifter. *That* was scary stuff. Being the center of someone's existence held a lot of responsibility.

"Logan certainly got the raw end of this deal. He's so, perfect, and I'm, well…I'm…just look at me." He looked down at his thin chest and abdomen. "How could he not be disappointed? I'm just—hey!" Keeton yelled, rubbing his forehead where Braxton had slapped him.

"Nice one, runt," Talon praised quietly.

"Shut the hell up, Keeton!" Braxton's eyes flashed with his anger. Keeton could not remember a time Braxton had ever been angry with him. Frustrated, exasperated, impatient, yes, but never angry.

"First, what the fuck do you mean no one's ever needed you? I've always needed you! Who took care of me and got me back on my feet when my family died in that fire? If it wasn't for you and your family, I don't know what would have happened to me!" Braxton leaned up on his knees and got right in Keeton's face.

He fought the urge to lean back and cover his ears. Damn,

Braxton was loud when he was pissed off. "And just for the record, I think Logan is damn lucky to have you as a mate. You are smart, funny, caring, and sexy as sin. Why wouldn't he want you? I don't ever want to hear that stupid shit come out of your mouth again. Understood?"

Keeton sat gaping at his best friend. Jackson and Boston were trying desperately not to laugh. Talon rolled his eyes, not bothering to hide his amusement. Xander...well, Xander looked like he might bend his little mate over the bed and fuck him unconscious.

"Fuck, it's hot when you get steamed up, baby." Xander's voice floated across the room, low and husky, practically dripping with desire. "Come on, *chulo,* or I'll take you here in front of everyone." He held open his arms, and Braxton jumped into them with a chuckle.

"Come on, big guy, I've got plenty more where that came from." Their lips locked, and Xander stumbled from the room with Braxton wrapped around him.

It hit Keeton in that moment. He wanted what Braxton and Xander had, and more importantly, he could have it. He needed to find Logan.

Jackson and Boston followed them out, still shaking with the effort to contain their laughter. Talon looked a Keeton for a long time before he spoke. "The runt is right, ya know. You are perfect for my brother." He turned to leave the room without further comment.

"Where's Logan?" Keeton called hurriedly.

"Running in the woods." Talon glanced back at him. "Be sure, Keeton." He nodded, and Talon left.

Chapter Seven

Keeton pushed his way through the trees and brush, looking for his mate. He no longer had to force himself to say the word. The rain fell from the sky, the sun rose in the east, and Logan was his mate.

He felt like he'd been wandering the woods for hours, and maybe he had. The sky darkened, and the breeze carried the scent of rain. He actually hoped Logan would come find him. Surely, the man could smell him. Hell, Keeton could smell himself. He was dirty and tired and ached everywhere. He hated nature.

Jackson and Boston had offered their help, but Keeton needed to do this on his own. The longer he stomped through the trees, the more he regretted the decision. As the sun began to set and the darkness swallowed up the land, he started to worry. He didn't know what roamed the woods at night, but his imagination had no qualms in conjuring up beasts of all kinds—mostly with long claws and razor-sharp teeth.

Keeton sighed, finally giving in to the fact that his tracking skills sucked. He would just go back to the house and wait for his mate there. Logan had to come home at some point. Turning to head back, he froze, whipping his head around. He spun in a circle, once, twice, a third time.

"Fuck! No, no, no!" Keeton groaned. At some point in his search, he had strayed from the path. He did not recognize anything, had no idea how far into the woods he had trekked. All he could see were trees.

Thunder rumbled in the distance, causing Keeton to whimper pathetically. It would be too much to hope that the storm would go around, or that he'd make it to shelter before it hit. He began walking again, hopefully in the direction of the house, and prayed that someone would come find him.

* * * *

Logan trudged up the front steps and stumbled through the door. He was cold, wet, and tired. When he left Keeton, he had fully intended to go for a run in the woods. He hadn't even made it to the back door before his phone rang, and he'd been called into work. One of the paramedics on the schedule had taken a nasty fall off his roof, breaking his leg in three places, and they needed him to fill in.

He had been thankful for the distraction from his thoughts surrounding his mate. Though a short shift, only six hours, it had been grueling—two car wrecks, a shooting, and a stroke. No one had died on Logan's watch, and he was both proud and grateful for the fact.

Now, he needed to talk to his mate. He had made a grand mess of this mating thing, and he just hoped Keeton would give him a chance to apologize. Maybe he didn't deserve Keeton's forgiveness, but he had to try.

"Where's Keeton?" Braxton asked as he walked into the room.

Logan had seen Keeton's car parked behind Jackson's when he drove up and assumed Keeton was still in the house. "Isn't he here?"

"No, he went looking for you." Braxton glared at him with his arms crossed over his chest.

"I got called in."

"Your Jeep has been here all day."

"Yeah, I took my bike, which would explain why I'm sopping wet. Ninety miles per hour on the back of a hog will do that." Logan didn't know why they were having this conversation. What did it matter what mode of transportation he used?

He watched as Braxton's arms fell limply to his sides, and his face paled. "Oh shit," Braxton whispered. "Xander!"

Xander came running down the stairs, closely followed by Jackson. "What, *chulo*? What's wrong?" He strode across the room and wrapped his arms securely around Braxton.

"Keeton," the little man said, his voice strained. "We have to find him."

"What the hell is going on?" Logan yelled. "Where the fuck is my mate?"

Braxton pushed Xander away and walked right up to Logan, pointing a finger into his chest. "You walked out and left him! We thought you'd gone to run in the woods, so that's what we told him. He left hours ago to go look for you! Now, he's out there alone in the dark, the rain, and he's probably scared to death." Braxton's voice had dropped to a horrified whisper by the time he finished. All the anger seemed to melt away, replaced by worry for his friend.

Logan couldn't breathe. His angel was out in the woods alone. He could hear the rain pounding against the roof. The thunder boomed and rolled as lightning flashed across the sky.

"Go find him!" Braxton shrieked.

Xander pulled his mate close and nuzzled his hair. "Shh, baby. We'll find him."

Logan started stripping his clothes off to shift before Xander even finished speaking.

"No!" Xander roared.

His attention snapped to Xander, and he watched the big alpha wrap his mate in his arms and turn him toward the staircase. *Shit!* He had completely forgotten that he could not shift in front of Braxton.

"Jackson, stay here and keep Braxton safe." Xander gave his mate a little push to get him moving.

Braxton nodded. "Just find him." Then he hurried up the stairs with Jackson following close behind.

With his alpha's mate out of the room, Logan closed his eyes and felt the heat spread through him as his beast took over. With the transformation complete, he opened his eyes and sprinted through the house to the back door. He skidded to a halt when he reached it, hissing and spitting at the doorknob.

Xander came right behind him, though, already starting to strip out of his clothes. He opened the door, and Logan shot out as if launched from a cannon. He knew Xander would shift and follow.

Sprinting across the backyard, he reached the edge of the woods in record time. He paced among the trees, sniffing the ground, trying to pick up his mate's scent. They owned all forty acres of the woods surrounding the house, and Logan would search every inch of it to find Keeton.

Just as panic began to set in because he couldn't pick up Keeton's scent, he heard a deep chuffing noise. He looked up from his frantic sniffing to find a huge white tiger standing a few yards down the tree line.

Logan gave a mental sigh, relieved his alpha had found the trail. He raced over, immediately picking up the scent, and charged in through the trees.

He didn't know how long they ran, didn't care, but eventually Keeton's scent became stronger. He quickened the pace, knowing they were getting close to his mate.

Logan stepped through the trees, into a small clearing, and sniffed the air. His steps faltered at the same time he heard Xander's deep growl. The scent of blood hung thick in the air. His feline eyes easily cut through the darkness, spotting Keeton curled up on his side next to a big boulder in the middle of the clearing.

Logan quickly shifted back to his human form and ran to his mate. He dropped to his knees and gripped Keeton's slim shoulder, carefully rolling him to his back. Logan's eyes filled with tears at the sight of his lover's body. Keeton's wet shirt clung to him in shreds. Four deep gashes ran diagonally from his left shoulder to his right hip bone. Blood pooled beneath his small body, swirling with the rain.

Logan reached out to cup his angel's face, his heart seizing when he found the skin cold. "No, no, no! Keeton, open your eyes, baby.

Keeton!" Logan pleaded. He moved his hand down Keeton's throat and almost passed out when relief slammed into him. Slow and faint, but a pulse beat beneath his fingers.

A strangled sob escaped him as he bent over and kissed Keeton's temple. "I'm going to take care of you, baby. You're going to be okay," Logan whispered into his mate's hair. "Please, open your eyes, Keeton."

His pleas received no reply, and he could barely feel the rise and fall of Keeton's chest. He turned when Xander stepped through the trees, also in his human form. "We need an ambulance."

Xander nodded once and hurried back out of the clearing. Gently pulling his lover into his arms, Logan cradled his broken body against his chest, and swiftly followed Xander into the trees.

The return trip through the woods took much longer, but he made steady progress. Just as he stepped through the last row of trees, a small moan drew his attention to the bundle in his arms.

"It's okay, baby. I've got you. We're going to get you fixed up. Just hold on, Keeton." Logan spoke softly, trying to reassure his mate. Inside, however, the panic gnawed at him. He desperately needed to get his angel to a doctor. Keeton had lost so much blood. His lips were blue, and his usually creamy skin looked pale and gray.

"Logan?" Keeton gurgled.

"I'm here, baby. Just rest."

"Hurts," he breathed weakly.

Logan felt tears prickle at the corners of his eyes, but he wouldn't allow them to fall. Keeton needed him to be strong. "Shh, I know, baby. We're almost there."

* * * *

"How's Braxton?" Logan asked into the phone as he continued pacing the waiting room. Keeton had been in surgery for over an hour, and the lack of news ate away at his patience.

"Better. Sleeping. Still nothing on Keeton?" Xander spoke quietly. Braxton had gone into hysterics when he saw Logan bring Keeton out of the woods. It had taken Xander nearly twenty minutes to calm his little mate and force him to take a sleeping pill.

"No. Nothing. Has anyone called his parents?" Logan ran a shaky hand over his face.

"I called, but there was no answer. I left a message for them to call back. Don't know what else to do."

"You've done everything you can. Thank you, Xander, for everything."

"Anytime. I'm going to check on Braxton, but call me if you need anything."

"I will. Thanks again." Logan disconnected and sat down heavily in one of the waiting room chairs.

"Logan?"

Jumping to his feet again, he crossed the waiting room, wrapping his arms around his partner and fellow paramedic, Carmen Mendoza. She hugged him back, smoothing her hands up and down his spine.

"Xander called. How is he?"

Logan released the petite woman and stepped away. "I don't know, Mendoza. He's still in surgery." Logan sighed. "You know they can't tell me anything anyway. I'm not family."

Mendoza took his hands in hers and squeezed. She gave him a small smile and a quick wink. "Rafe is working ICU tonight. Just leave it to me."

Logan smiled. Rafael Mendoza was Carmen's husband and one of the doctors at the hospital. "I love you."

Mendoza patted his shoulder. "I know. C'mon, they'll move him to ICU once he's out of recovery. Let's go up and wait there." She pulled him along as she made her way to the elevator.

Logan followed along in a kind of stupor. He couldn't remember ever being so scared in his life. If Keeton died, Logan would never forgive himself. Keeton had been in the woods in the first place because of him. If he hadn't left, Keeton wouldn't have gone looking for him, and his mate would not be in the hospital, fighting for his life.

Obviously, something had attacked Keeton out in the woods. Logan couldn't even begin to imagine what could have ripped open his mate like that. Neither he nor Xander had picked up any scent in that clearing other than Keeton's. Besides, Keeton hadn't been mauled or bitten. He had no other injuries besides the gashes on his chest. It didn't make any sense, and Logan was too exhausted to think.

"Sit here and rest. I'll be right back." Mendoza gave him a gentle shove.

Logan hadn't even realized they had made it to the ICU waiting room. He didn't argue, but flopped down on the love seat, covered his face with his hands, and finally let himself go.

Chapter Eight

Keeton woke to the sound of raised voices. He didn't know whom the female voice belonged to, but he recognized the deep, masculine voice immediately.

"Logan?" Keeton rasped hoarsely.

Logan appeared at his side instantly. He took Keeton's hand—the one not hooked up to an IV—and squeezed gently. "I'm right here, angel. How are you feeling?"

"Hurts," Keeton whispered. He hurt everywhere. He knew he was in a hospital, but he couldn't remember why. Whatever the reason, he knew it had been awful. Nothing could be this painful and not be bad.

Keeton reached up to wrap his arms around Logan's neck and gasped. His stomach ached and burned, the pain radiating clear through his body. His back arched, and he cried out.

"Easy, easy, baby. Don't move. I'm right here, and I'm not going anywhere." Logan placed a gentle kiss on Keeton's brow.

"Mr. Cartwright, I'm sorry, but visiting hours are over. Unless you are family, I'm going to have to ask you to leave." That annoying feminine voice was back.

"I'm not leaving," Logan stated firmly, never looking away from Keeton.

"Mr. Cartwright, please, I'll be forced to call security if you do not leave." Keeton disliked her immediately. She would not take Logan away from him.

"No."

"Mr. Taylor." Now the irritating voice addressed him. "I'm sorry, but visiting hours are over. Mr. Cart—"

"No," Keeton interrupted her. "He is my husband, and I want him here." Keeton squeezed Logan's hand when the big man gasped in surprise. Logan had his back to the nurse, so she missed the look of shock on his handsome face. Keeton had the insane urge to giggle.

The dragon-lady crossed her arms and narrowed her eyes at the couple on the bed. "I don't think—"

"I do." Keeton glared right back at the aging nurse. "If he were my *wife*, you wouldn't have any problem with him being here, and we both know it."

She huffed once, before turning on her heels and storming from the room.

Keeton returned his attention to his mate, surprised to see a smile flitting over Logan's lips. "You are incredible," Logan murmured.

"How long have I been in the hospital? *Why* am I in the hospital? What happened?" Keeton frowned.

"You don't remember anything?" When he shook his head, Logan closed his eyes briefly and sighed. "You've been in ICU for four days. You lost a lot of blood, and your wounds were infected. They've been keeping you sedated. If you do well tonight, they're going to move you to a regular room tomorrow."

Keeton looked down and noticed the white gauze wrapped around his bare torso. "What the hell happened to me?" he gasped.

"Do you remember anything?"

He wrinkled his nose in concentration. "I went out in the woods to look for you. It got dark, and then it started to rain. That's the last thing I remember before waking up here." Keeton looked into Logan's eyes. "Where were you?"

"Oh, baby, I got called into work. I'm so, so sorry. I should have never left you like that. It will never happen again. I swear to you."

Keeton couldn't help but trust the sincerity in Logan's voice. He smiled up at his lover. "Already forgiven. Now, shut up and kiss me."

"Anything you want, angel," Logan whispered. He leaned down and pressed his mouth tenderly to Keeton's dry lips. The kiss was brief, chaste, but the sweetest kiss Keeton had ever received.

He sighed when Logan sat back. He would have been happy to go on kissing the man, but he needed answers. "So, you said I had an infection?"

"It was almost like you were poisoned. I've never been so damn scared in my life," Logan answered shakily. His voice cracked twice.

Keeton reached for Logan again, but stopped, frowning at the needle in his hand. "Need to hold you," he mumbled.

Logan took his shoes and shirt off, then slowly and gently maneuvered them both so that he lay in the bed beside him. He took Keeton's unencumbered hand and brought it to his face. "Better? Is this okay? You don't hurt anywhere?"

Keeton smiled. His big, strong mate really was too wonderful for words. "Better than okay. Thank you."

* * * *

"Do you need anything? Are you hungry? Water?"

Keeton rolled his eyes and sighed. Logan had been flapping around him like a mother hen since his release from the hospital two weeks before. His lover's concern and attention had been nice at first, but it quickly began to smother him. Secretly, he would be glad when Logan left for work.

"I'm fine, Logan. Really. It barely twinges anymore, and I haven't even taken a pain pill in two days." Keeton tried for reassuring, but feared it came off more as annoyed and exasperated.

Logan frowned. "Are you sure? I can call in, baby."

"Logan! You haven't been to work since I came home. Stop hovering and go already!" Keeton snapped.

He regretted his words almost immediately when he saw the hurt look on Logan's face. "Ah, Logan, I'm sorry." Keeton ran his fingers through his short hair. "Come here." He held his arms out, relieved when Logan crawled into bed beside him without hesitation.

"I'm sorry, too," Logan whispered. He gently wound his arms around Keeton and held him close. "You don't know what it was like. I was scared out of my mind that I was going to lose you. I get scared all over again every time I have to leave you. I'll try to be better, promise."

Keeton blinked rapidly, banishing the tears he felt coming. He knew he'd be acting the same way in Logan's position. He couldn't imagine what he would do if he ever lost his mate. He didn't even want to think about it.

As his body continued to heal, Logan refused to do more than snuggle and kiss. Keeton understood, even if his body didn't. He felt damn frustrated at times, though.

So, instead, they had spent a lot of time talking, getting to know one another. Everything Keeton learned about Logan had him falling for the man that much more.

Logan lived to help people, make their lives better, easier. He cooked, played guitar, and was obsessed with old slasher movies. He had even brought a television up to his room so that they could cuddle and watch some of his collection in bed.

Keeton squeezed his mate tighter, kissed the top of his head, then pushed him away gently and smiled. "Go to work. Braxton will keep me company and be my manservant for the night."

Logan rubbed their noses together and grinned. "Okay." He rolled from the bed and headed toward the door. "Do you need me to get anything from your place before I come home?"

Keeton turned his head to hide his smirk. It hadn't escaped his notice that his things had been slowly making their way from his cottage to the house he now shared with Braxton and the pack. He loved his cottage, but his place was with Logan. He'd have to call a realtor in the morning. "Nah, I'm good. We'll just pack it all up and move it over here on your next day off."

"Really?" Logan looked like Christmas had come early.

Keeton chuckled. "Yes, really. I belong with you, and you need to be with the pack, so..." He trailed off, opening his arms wide.

Logan raced across the room and planted a searing kiss on Keeton's lips. "You belong with me."

"That's what I just said, dummy, now shoo!"

Logan laughed a deep, belly-rumbling laugh, an extra hop in his step as he left the room.

Chapter Nine

His call went straight to voice mail for the third time that week. Keeton frowned, ended the call without leaving a message, and dialed again.

"Hello?"

"Hey, Blaise, it's your favorite cousin," he teased.

"Anna's my favorite cousin, dipshit." Blaise laughed at his own joke. "Good to hear from you, man. How's it going?"

"Pretty great actually. I mated a shifter." Keeton said it with such ease that he surprised himself. It had become just another part of his life. He had blond hair, a birthmark on his right ankle, and he had mated a shifter.

"What?" Blaise yelled. "Holy damn, Keeton! Well…is he hot?"

Keeton giggled. Man, he missed his cousin. "Blaise, you aren't even gay! But oh, yeah, he's gorgeous!"

"Right on. Score!" Blaise whooped, drawing more laughter from Keeton.

They talked for a while longer about what Keeton had been doing, about Logan, and about Blaise's latest adventures. His cousin's journeys around the world never failed to amaze him. He still didn't know exactly what Blaise did for a living, but it sounded exciting, if not a little dangerous.

"Hey, Blaise, the reason I called is, well, I was wondering if you'd talked to my parents? I've been trying to call them for almost two weeks now, and I just keep getting voice mail."

When Logan had first told him that they could not get in touch with his parents, Keeton hadn't thought much of it. His parents were always off on some new undertaking, and sometimes it would be months before he heard from them.

"Eh, well, no. Uh, Keeton, when was the last time you talked to your parents?" Blaise's voice sounded strained.

"It's been almost four weeks, I guess. Why?"

"Is everything okay? Is there a reason you need to get in touch with them?" Blaise answered Keeton's question with one of his own.

Keeton told Blaise about being attacked by some unknown animal in the woods, his time spent in the hospital, the infection, everything. He assured his cousin he was doing fine and healing well. "It's just weird that I can't get in touch with them, and it has me worried," he finished.

"An animal?" Blaise sounded more like he was talking to himself than to Keeton. "Did you fight with anyone before you were attacked?"

"Just Logan, but he would never hurt me," Keeton replied defensively. "Oh, and that bitch of an ex-girlfriend of his," he spat.

"Was there anything strange about the girlfriend?"

"*Ex*-girlfriend, and yes, actually. She didn't have an aura. Well, she did, sort of, but it didn't have a core. It was as if she didn't have a soul. Then she went on about how Logan belonged to her, and she lied about being pregnant. Oh, and I don't think Logan can scent her emotions. I mean, he'd be able to tell if she was lying just from her scent, right?"

"Keeton, I want you to stay where you are. Do not leave that house for any reason. I'll be there as soon as I can, which will probably be about three days." Blaise spoke quickly, his voice tense and worried.

"Why? What the hell is going on?"

"Just don't leave that house! Promise me!" Blaise yelled.

"Fine, but—" Keeton jerked back and looked at the phone when Blaise hung up on him.

Well hell, that certainly had not gone as planned. He still didn't have any news about his parents, and now someone that didn't even live there had placed him under house arrest. Add to that Blaise's reaction to his ramblings about Mariah. He had sounded angry, but also a little worried.

Keeton needed to talk to Logan. He punched in the speed dial for his cell phone and waited.

* * * *

Logan stood in the back of his rig, checking supplies, and restocking where necessary. He pulled his phone from his pocket when it rang and frowned when he saw Keeton's name on the caller ID.

"Keeton? Baby, what's wrong?" Logan asked worriedly. "Do you need me to come home?"

Keeton's giggle eased the knot in his chest. "No, I'm fine. You've been at work for what, two hours?"

Logan smiled. Yeah, he knew he sounded overprotective, but he couldn't change his nature. "Okay, so what's up?"

"I needed to let you know that my cousin, Blaise, is coming to visit. He's a shifter, and I don't really know the protocol. Do I need to get Xander's permission?" Keeton talked so quickly, Logan could barely understand him.

"Whoa. Slow down, angel. Now, who's coming to visit?"

"My cousin, Blaise," Keeton answered a bit slower.

"And, you said he is a shifter?"

"Yes, and I was wondering if I needed to get Xander's permission, what with him being the alpha, and this being his territory."

Logan thought for a moment before he answered. "It would probably be a good idea to let Xander know, but you don't exactly have to ask his permission." He paused again then asked, "What kind of shifter is your cousin?"

"Eh, a wolf," Keeton responded. "What do you shift into, Logan?"

"A snow leopard," he mumbled. He really didn't want to have this conversation over the phone. Keeton knew quite a bit about shifters, but not about Logan's particular breed. They would need to have that conversation soon, just not now.

"What?" Keeton sounded curious, nothing else.

"A snow leopard," Logan repeated more clearly.

"Oh, no shit? That's awesome! I bet you are gorgeous. When can I see you shift?"

Logan fell into a shocked silence. He had to remind himself that his little mate didn't understand the curse he lived with as a white-pelted shifter. His kind had been hunted for as long as he could remember…sometimes by their own families.

"I will show you whenever you want."

"Yay! Okay, I'll let you get back to work."

Logan chuckled at his lover's enthusiasm. "I'll see you when I get home." He glanced at his watch and groaned. "In eight more hours."

"Can you call me on your break? You get a break, right?"

"My break is in about three hours. I'll talk to you then, unless I'm out on a call."

"Can't wait. Later." Then the call disconnected.

Logan grinned and slid his phone back into his pocket. Keeton embodied everything he had ever wanted in a mate. He had a big heart, a kind soul, and a zest for life that often left Logan stumbling to keep up.

He didn't understand half the things Keeton said sometimes, but he listened with rapt attention, enjoying the animation in his mate's voice, the excitement on his face.

Logan couldn't wait to get home.

Chapter Ten

"You can't hide forever, honey."

Keeton glared at his best friend. "I'm not hiding anything, Brax. I don't know what you're talking about."

Keeton already felt out of sorts because Logan had never called him back. Yes, his mate had a job to do, but that didn't mean he had to like it. A few hours before, he had been happy to see Logan leaving, but now, he missed him like crazy.

"You know *exactly* what I'm talking about." Braxton's voice brought him out of his thoughts. "Logan will love you no matter what, Keeton. You need to stop pretending to be something you're not."

"What the hell is that supposed to mean?" he snapped.

Braxton sighed and threw his hands up in frustration. "Will you just cut the bullshit? You've been wearing my clothes. I found all of your makeup in the trash, and you haven't painted your nails in weeks. You pretend to like those gross slasher flicks, and you ate a fucking hamburger last night. Since when do you eat meat?" Braxton was on a roll, and Keeton didn't think he'd get a word in any time soon.

"Hell, even the way you talk has changed," Braxton ranted. "I haven't heard one smartass comment out of your mouth since you came home from the hospital. You're driving me insane!" He paused to take a deep breath. "I want my best friend back, Keeton," he added, his tone almost pleading.

Keeton didn't know how to respond. What could he say? Braxton had said it all.

"What if he doesn't like me? I mean, the me that I usually am," he whispered.

"Then he doesn't deserve you, honey." Braxton gave him a crooked grin and patted Keeton's bent knee. "If you keep this up, you're just going to be miserable. You and Logan both deserve better than that. Have a little faith in your mate."

Keeton leaned back against his pillows and sighed. "He's not like anyone I've ever dated, Brax. There's the fact that he's just so…so…huge! He's big, and tough, and strong, but he's also sweet, kind, and gentle. He's the essence of goodness, and he makes me want to be a better person. Am I making any sense?"

Braxton's grin widened, and he nodded. "I know what you mean. I feel the same way about Xander." He moved up the bed to lean against the headboard beside Keeton. "And it's okay to want to be a better person, Kee, but that doesn't mean that you have to change everything about yourself. I think you're pretty fantastic just the way you are." Braxton winked at him.

Keeton snorted and rolled his eyes. "I love you, Brax, even if you are an ass sometimes."

Braxton laughed and nudged Keeton's shoulder with his own. "Love ya, too, even if you are a whiney bitch sometimes." He eased off the bed and walked to the door. "Be back in a sec," he called over his shoulder as he disappeared down the hallway.

Less than a minute later, he waltzed back into the room, carrying a big blue makeup case that looked a lot like a small tackle box. He sat the case on the bed, flipped the latches, and opened it up.

Keeton's eyes widened, and his face split into a huge grin. He stared into the case filled with everything from eyeliner to fingernail polish. It even held wax and cloth strips, and a box of hair bleach.

"I know it's not your birthday or Christmas," Braxton shrugged, "but I figured you needed this now." He looked into Keeton's eyes, then cocked his head to the side. "So, what do you say, Kee?"

Braxton got him. He understood all of Keeton's little quirks and idiosyncrasies, and loved him *because* of them, not in spite of them.

"Could you help me dye my hair? I just know my roots are a mess."

Braxton beamed at him and nodded. "Sure, but I'm not helping you wax your balls, dude. That's all you."

* * * *

Logan pulled into his driveway and turned off the engine ten minutes before midnight. He sat in his Jeep, just staring at the house through his windshield.

He grinned and felt his heart flutter. He couldn't believe in a few short days, Keeton would live here permanently. Never in his life had he been happier or more content. He had dreamed of finding the perfect mate since he learned what the word meant.

Logan hadn't been with many men, always preferring the soft, petite build of a woman. Women found his size and physique a turn-on, and they played to his need to be dominant and in control.

Men, on the other hand, either felt intimidated by his size, or looked at it as a challenge for authority. Keeton did neither.

He seemed happy to let Logan be in charge and control the more physical aspects of their relationship. He never failed to make his opinions known, though. His mate would not hesitate to hand Logan his ass on a silver platter if he stepped out of line.

He loved that about his mate. None of his lovers—men or women—had been able to navigate that narrow line. Keeton had the ability to assert himself, while still acknowledging Logan's status as alpha in their relationship.

In the short time since fate had thrown Keeton in his path, he had become the center of Logan's world. He exemplified everything Logan ever imagined his mate to be. Warm, kind, and sexy, his body soft and yielding, his skin pale and supple, the man personified sex. Though not necessarily feminine, no one would call him the poster boy for masculinity either.

Add charming, witty, and intelligent to his list of attributes, and Keeton was the total package.

Logan looked up to the second floor and smiled when he saw the light in his and Keeton's bedroom through the window. His mate waited up for him.

He never found time to call Keeton back. His stomach rumbled, reminding him that he had not found the time to eat either.

Summer had officially arrived. The months between the last day of school and the beginning of a new year were always long and grueling. Logan would be spending a lot of time making runs out to the lake, or one of the several community pools.

Then, he had to survive the Fourth of July. The entire weekend would be insane, but the Fourth, itself, would be downright miserable. It raced towards him with alarming speed. Only two weeks remained of June. Sometimes he wished he had chosen a different profession.

A sharp rap of knuckles on his window made Logan jump. He whipped around to find his brother frowning at him. Nodding, he gathered his things, opened the door, and climbed out of the SUV.

"What's up?"

"Mariah came by tonight," Talon answered promptly.

Logan ground his teeth together and fought back his anger. "What did she want?" he asked as calmly as possible. Then another thought occurred to him. "Oh, shit, Keeton didn't see her, did he?"

Talon shook his head, stuffing his hands in the pockets of his jeans. "No, she didn't make it past the front door, bro. I wouldn't do that to you."

He clapped his brother on the back affectionately. "I know, Tal. Thank you. So, what was she after?"

"Uh, well…" Talon trailed off, obviously uncomfortable. A rare expression for him, and it immediately put Logan on alert.

"Talon?"

"Well, I think she was after me."

Logan almost laughed. Almost. Talon looked so confused, so

uneasy, that he choked down his amusement. He had caught Mariah staring at Talon a time or two, but just assumed it was the whole twin thing. He couldn't count the number of times someone approached them with offers of a threesome. Though not identical, they looked enough alike to count.

"It was creepy, man. She asked if you were here, and when I told her no, she just kind of leered at me. Like she was going to eat me, ya know?" Talon glared at the ground.

Logan knew the feeling. "So, then what happened?"

"Hell, I don't know. I'm telling her she needs to leave, and she's got her hands all over me. Then she starts rubbing up against me like a cat in heat. I swear, I thought she was going to hump my leg right there on the porch."

Logan chuckled darkly. "She's a piece of work, huh? I don't know what I ever saw in her."

"Well, she's hot as fuck, I'll give you that. She's damn weird, though." Talon shook his head. "Then Jackson came to the door, and she's eyeing him like he's the special on the menu." Talon growled, his anger clear on his face.

Logan didn't know what to make of that, so he dismissed it. He had other things to worry about. "What happened then?"

"Well, I told the kid to beat it, so he went and tattled to Xander apparently. Xander comes to the door, and Mariah is all turning on the charm for him." This time, Talon laughed.

Interesting.

"She's all pressed up against him, smiling and purring. Then..." Talon laughed again and shook his head. "Then, Braxton walks in. Damn, that runt is a pistol. It took me and Xander both to hold him back."

Logan laughed along with his brother. He could just picture Braxton trying to rip Mariah's hair out of her head for daring to touch his mate.

"No one has told Keeton," Talon continued seriously. "I think he needs to know, though. There's something not right about that woman, my brother."

Logan nodded his agreement. "I'll tell him. I don't think she's dangerous, but it's better for him to be on his guard."

Talon nodded as well. "Good. I'm going for a run. I'll see you later."

Logan watched him take off around the house and head for the forest, and fought back the need to follow or call him back. Something dangerous lurked out in the woods. He knew his brother was bigger and stronger than Keeton, and could take care of himself, but he still worried.

Glancing back up at his bedroom window, he sighed when he saw the light off. Apparently, Keeton had gotten tired of waiting for him and gone to bed.

Then, before he could take a step, he heard the man yell from inside the house. Body tensing, preparing to defend his mate, he raced up the porch steps and barreled through the front door. The sight that greeted him froze his feet to the floor. He growled softly, but didn't move any closer.

Keeton lay on his back, spread out on the living room floor, naked from the waist down. Jackson knelt between his legs, looking down at him. Neither noticed Logan's arrival.

"Fuck!" Jackson yelled. "Are you okay, Keeton? I don't want to do this anymore. Why the hell would you ever do this?"

Yeah, that's what Logan wanted to know. Why the hell would Keeton be messing around with Jackson? How could he do this to him?

"We're almost done, Jacks. Just one more," Keeton panted.

Huh? One more what? Obviously, Logan had missed something. He remained silent, keeping to the dark entryway, watching.

"Keeton, I don't want to," Jackson whined. "I don't like hurting you."

"It doesn't really hurt that bad," Keeton assured him. "Just do it, and hurry up about it. Logan will be home soon, and I still have to go shower."

Logan eyed the pair curiously, watching as Jackson picked up a small jar, twirled something around in it that looked like a tongue depressor, and smeared the yellowish goop over Keeton's sac.

He had to choke back another growl at the sight of another man touching his mate so intimately. The only thing saving Jackson from an ass beating was that he obviously didn't want to be doing it. Logan could not detect even a trace scent of arousal from either of them.

Jackson took a long strip of white cloth and smoothed it over the goo. Logan gaped, clarity working its way through his jealousy. *Sweet hell, he's waxing Keeton's scrotum.*

"Why can't you do this yourself?" Jackson still sounded whiney and uncomfortable.

"I can't bend like I need to without pulling the stitches in my chest," Keeton said irritably. "Just do it, and remember to pull the skin tight, or you'll rip my balls off."

Other than the fact that another man fondled his mate's balls, Logan thought it was the funniest thing he had ever witnessed. He continued to watch from the shadows as Jackson pulled Keeton's skin taut, took a deep breath, then yanked sharply on the strip of fabric. Logan bit his lip and winced in sympathy as his balls shrank and tried to crawl up inside him.

Keeton yelled again, and his body bowed up off the floor. Jackson hurriedly backed away and stood to his feet. "No more, Keeton. Don't ever ask me to do that shit again!" He glared down at the little man, then sprinted from the room.

Logan could not agree more. Although not enthusiastic about causing Keeton pain, he would damn sure be the one to help his mate the next time. No one should ever see Keeton like that, or touch is lithe body, other than Logan.

Keeton took several deep breaths, rose from the floor, gathered the mess, and left the room.

Logan sighed as Keeton made his way up the stairs. It sounded like his angel had something planned, and he didn't want to ruin the surprise. He would give Keeton a few more minutes before he went to find him.

In the meantime, he needed to have a word with Jackson.

He found the youngest brother in the kitchen, wreaking havoc on a package of Oreos. Jackson tensed when he saw him walk into the room, guilt written all over his face.

"Uh, hey, Logan, when did you get home?"

"Oh, just a few minutes ago," he answered, smiling.

Jackson gulped audibly, and he looked a little green. Then he started babbling a mile a minute. "I'm so sorry, Logan. I didn't want to do it. Keeton asked me if I would help him, and I said yes, but I didn't know what he wanted me to do. I promise we didn't do anything, and I don't even like him like that. Oh, shit, Logan, don't kill me."

Logan had to laugh. All his anger melted away, and he ruffled Jackson's hair. "Calm down, kid. I'm not going to kill you. I have to admit, I thought about it when I first walked in the door, but I'm okay now. It won't happen again, though. Clear?"

Jackson nodded enthusiastically, his head bobbing like a jackhammer. "No problem. I never want to do that again. How in the fuck can he stand it? It makes my balls burn just thinking about it."

Logan chuckled again at the bewildered look on Jackson's face. "Well, it's not something I'd want done to me either." He glanced up toward the ceiling. "So, how long do you think I should give him?"

Relaxing a little more, Jackson rolled his eyes and shrugged. "I'd say at least another ten minutes. He's kind of…high maintenance, huh?"

Logan just shook his head. "I think he's perfect."

"Well, of course *you* do." Jackson snorted. He put away the cookies and turned for the back door. "I'm going to run. Later." He gave a little wave and disappeared into the night.

Chapter Eleven

After Logan inhaled a couple of sandwiches to appease his aching stomach, he cleaned up the kitchen and went to find his mate. Surely, he had given Keeton enough time.

He climbed the stairs to the room they shared, pushed open the door, and almost fell to his knees.

Keeton sprawled on his back in the middle of the bed, wearing absolutely nothing. His gelled spikes appeared newly dyed, so blond they looked almost white.

Logan moved closer to the bed, his legs shaking, and his body trembling. Black eyeliner circled his mate's bright blue eyes. His pink lips glimmered, slick and shiny, and Logan longed to taste them. Electric-blue nail polish adorned his fingernails and toenails, standing out in sharp relief against his smooth, creamy skin.

Keeton traced his fingers lightly across the still-healing wounds on his chest. "There's not much I can do about these. I know they're not pretty." He stopped speaking and shrugged. His other hand moved down his bare torso to cup his freshly waxed sac. "Nothing wrong here though." He grinned impishly.

Logan couldn't speak. Keeton had been gorgeous before, but now Logan was afraid to let his little mate leave the house. He would be fighting off would-be suitors left and right. Did Keeton normally look like this? Had he been holding this part of himself back from Logan?

"Logan, please say something." Keeton sounded nervous, and Logan could see the quiet quivering of his body.

He pulled his uniform off quickly, his eyes never leaving Keeton. Making his way to the bed, he carefully slid in beside his angel, cupped Keeton's jaw in his hand, and placed a gentle kiss against his cheek. "You look absolutely edible, baby." He ground his erection against his lover's hip to emphasize his point. "Why haven't I seen you like this before?"

* * * *

Keeton took a deep breath and let it out slowly. *Here goes nothing.* "If I'm going to let you claim me," he ignored Logan's shallow gasp, "and if we're going to be truly mated, then I want you to know what you're getting yourself into."

Maneuvering himself onto his side, he propped up on one elbow to face Logan. "I'm stubborn, overemotional, and too sensitive for my own good. I'm a bit too...much for some people. I like to push the limits, and I'm the epitome of typical stereotypes about gay men. I like to sing, dance, and cook. I enjoy taking care of the people I love, and I think I would probably die if I couldn't draw or paint anymore."

Keeton didn't even give Logan a chance to respond. He had to get it all out before he choked on the words. "I'm a vegetarian, and that hamburger I nibbled at last night was the first animal I've eaten in almost nine years. I don't really like your slasher movies, and I don't understand a word you're saying when you talk about your motorcycle."

He held up his hand when it seemed that Logan would interrupt. "I think the gym is one step below the seventh circle of Hell, and I hate all those things guys are supposed to love, like sports, fishing, camping, and beer." Keeton shuddered. "I like to wear makeup and paint my nails."

He leaned in closer to Logan and placed a hand on his mate's chest, right over his heart. "I also believe in fairy tales, falling too fast, too hard, and living happily-ever-after." Now came the hard part. "And if you'll let me," he whispered, "if you still want me, I will love you for the rest of my life. No one will ever love you like I do,

Logan."

Keeton eased back and waited for his lover's reaction. He had unloaded everything on Logan, and it was a lot to absorb. Braxton was right, though. He would never be happy if he could not truly be himself.

Logan looked at him for a long time, his face expressionless. Then he leaned forward and kissed Keeton so tenderly that he felt tears well up in his eyes. He didn't know if it was a kiss of acceptance, or a kiss of good-bye.

"Boston is a vegetarian as well, so you two can work out what to feed yourselves around here," Logan began. "I will let you pick which movies we watch from now on, though I'd prefer no documentaries or anything where I have to read subtitles."

Keeton couldn't believe it. Logan accepted him, all of him. He didn't ask him to change or go back to being *normal*.

"I think you look sexy as sin with the eyeliner and nail polish, and I hope you wear them more often. I adore the fact that you want to take care of me because, well, frankly, I need it. I can't sing or dance, but I'm pretty good in the kitchen. I love all those things you hate, like sports and camping."

Logan kissed the tip of Keeton's nose and smiled. "But, I love you more. I want to spend the rest of our lives showing you just how much."

Keeton bit his lip to keep it from trembling. No one had ever loved him, accepted him, so unconditionally before. Well, except Braxton, but he didn't count.

He threw his arms around Logan's neck, buried his face into the warm skin of his throat, and cried. He cried because Logan loved him, because he wanted to be with him, and because he didn't want to change him.

Logan's arms wrapped around him and pulled him closer. He cupped the back of Keeton's head and just held him.

The smell of Logan's skin, combined with the warm weight of his naked body pressed against Keeton's, had him moaning and squirming against his mate within seconds. It had been too long since Logan had touched him.

"I need you, Logan. I need you to touch me, to make love to me. Please, love. Don't say no," he whispered into the hollow of Logan's throat. He caressed his lover's spine with the tips of his fingers, and smiled when he felt him shiver.

Logan rolled him gently to his back and hovered over him, careful to keep his full weight off of Keeton. He stared down at him with such intensity that Keeton couldn't contain his shudder of need. Then he smiled, bright enough to rival the sun. "I love you, angel."

"Why do you call me that?"

"Angel? Because you are my miracle. My sweet…pure…perfect angel." Logan punctuated each word with little kisses along Keeton's cheek and jawline.

His brain fogged, and his breathing sped slightly. "M'kay," he sighed. Who was he to argue anyway?

"I'm sorry for the way I treated you our first time. I wish I could take it back, but I promise, I'll do everything I can to make it up to you."

Keeton looked up at him in confusion. He had practically begged Logan for everything the man had done to him. How had Logan mistreated him? He started to ask, but all thoughts fled when Logan crushed his mouth down on his in a hungry kiss. Logan nipped and licked at his mouth coaxingly, seeking entrance. Keeton opened with a moan, slanting his mouth, and taking the kiss deeper.

Logan's unique taste exploded across his tongue and set his pulse racing. Keeton easily slipped into the submissive role, craving the feeling of security, turning his pleasure over to his lover.

"Please," he gasped, breaking the kiss. "Please, sir, touch me. I need you to touch me."

Logan leaned away and frowned at him. "You don't have to call me sir."

Keeton grinned. His mate really was too cute sometimes. "You love it when I call you sir. You like being in control, Logan. I know you do. You love that I'm submissive. If I don't like something, I will tell you." He pulled his lover back to him. "Now," he whispered against Logan's lips, "just shut up and do what feels right."

Logan looked at him for a long time before he spoke. "If I do anything, anything at all…"

Keeton placed his hand over Logan's mouth and smiled. "I'll tell you."

Logan nodded, and the look on his face became predatory. "You asked for it, angel." He growled seductively.

Yes! He had definitely asked for it, and he couldn't wait to get it. Reaching a hand beneath his pillow, he produced a bottle of lube and a pair of handcuffs. He smirked up at Logan as he presented his offerings.

Logan took the bottle of lube, but raised an eyebrow at the handcuffs. He took them from Keeton's hands and dropped them over the side of the bed. Keeton pouted in disappointment.

Logan chuckled and kissed his bottom lip. "Not to worry, angel." He levered himself to kneel beside Keeton, and patted his hip. "Roll over, baby."

Keeton complied eagerly, maybe too eagerly. He flung himself onto his stomach and hissed as his chest pressed against the sheets. The slashes across his body burned straight through to his spine. He bit his lip, trying desperately to power his way through the pain. If Logan knew he was hurting, everything would stop.

* * * *

Logan placed his hand between Keeton's shoulder blades and felt the muscles tense and bunch beneath his palm. "Keeton?"

He didn't answer, but Logan could hear his teeth grinding together. "Angel, what's wrong?"

Still, Keeton refused to answer. He shook his head, and Logan saw the flush of his face, the sweat beading across his forehead. Inhaling deeply, Logan grimaced when he caught the scent of his mate's blood. He pulled gently on Keeton's shoulder, then a little more insistently when he resisted him.

"Keeton," Logan commanded when he continued to fight him, "turn over and look at me." He didn't want to be harsh with his mate, but it got the job done.

Keeton sighed shakily as he slowly rolled over onto his back. His blood dotted the sheets and smeared thinly across his chest and stomach. Logan's own blood drained from his face, and he winced. When the hell would he get this mating thing right? He had done nothing but cause Keeton pain since they had met.

Three of Keeton's stitches had popped, and the puckered flesh around his wounds looked red and angry. Blood continued to trickle slowly down his chest.

"Oh, baby, I'm so sorry," Logan whispered. He stood from the bed and walked slowly toward the door.

"Logan Cartwright, if you leave me again, I promise you, I will not be responsible for my actions!" Keeton's angry voice vibrated through the room.

Logan actually smiled at his mate's vehemence. He turned around and held up his hands, palms out. "I'm just going to get a washcloth to clean you up. I will be right back, baby."

Keeton eyed him suspiciously for a second before he nodded. "Okay."

Logan rushed down the hall to the bathroom, wet a clean cloth with warm water, and rummaged in the medicine cabinet for gauze and tape. When he walked back in the room, Keeton seemed to be more relaxed, and the bleeding had stopped. Logan sighed in relief.

"Does it still hurt?" he asked as he sat on the side of the bed by his mate.

"Not as much." Keeton bit his lip and blushed. "I guess I should have added that I'm a klutz to that list I gave you earlier."

Logan just smiled indulgently at his lover as he gently cleaned the blood from Keeton's skin. He looked the wounds over, checking for infection. Thankfully, everything looked fine. The skin around the stitches felt warm, but not fevered. When he finished, he applied gauze pads to the wounds and taped them securely with surgical tape.

"This will be fine for now, but we're going to go see the doctor in the morning." He gave Keeton a stern look. There would be no argument.

Keeton smiled and nodded at him. "Thank you," he whispered.

"Anytime, baby, but please try to be more careful." Logan disposed of the trash and tossed the cloth toward the hamper before sliding into bed and curling around his lover.

Keeton opened his mouth to argue, but Logan silenced him with a quick kiss. "Not until the stitches come out. Now, go to sleep."

* * * *

Eleven days later, Keeton's stitches were removed. The skin still looked pink and puckered, but the doctor assured them everything was healing nicely.

Practically throwing his nude mate on the bed, Logan wanted to dance for joy. His self-imposed celibacy held little appeal to him, and he couldn't wait to celebrate its demise.

Trailing his fingertips over Keeton's hip and along his thigh, he smiled as the pretty little cock perked right up, waving hello to him. Well, maybe not so little. Keeton's cock was nice and thick, the skin smooth and pale, and Logan wanted to taste him.

"It's been too long," he murmured to his mate, running his tongue over the crease where Keeton's thigh met his groin.

Keeton arched up into his mouth and moaned. "Logan, please!"

Taking his mate's cries as agreement, he swiped his tongue up Keeton's long shaft then swirled it around the tip, catching the oozing drops of pre-cum that pooled there. Logan groaned at the flavors that zinged across his taste buds. Damn, his baby tasted amazing—rich and spicy, sweet and bitter, salty and tangy, all mixed together.

He swirled his tongue around the head again, then wrapped his lips firmly around the turgid flesh, and sucked hard.

Keeton came up off the bed, crying out and plunging his hands into Logan's hair. "Oh, my God!"

Logan smiled around Keeton's prick. He slid his lips down his mate's shaft until he buried his nose against his groin. He swallowed the crown, massaging it with his throat muscles, delighting in his lover's moans and whimpers.

He continued to lavish Keeton's shaft with his lips, his tongue, and his teeth. Just as he really started to get into it, humping his own throbbing cock against the mattress, Keeton yanked his head back roughly.

"Fuck me," he panted. "Please, Logan…oh, damn…please."

No man alive could resist such open pleading. Logan crawled to his knees between his lover's legs and reached for the bottle of lube on the nightstand. Grabbing two pillows, he quickly insinuated them beneath Keeton's hips.

"If I hurt you…"

"Shut the hell up and fuck me, damn it!" Keeton snarled.

Logan stared in awe. Wow, that was hot. He nodded sharply, lubed up his straining cock, and pushed two lubed fingers into his mate. He held his fingers still as Keeton's muscles clamped around him, and he gasped, his back bowing as he clutched at the sheets.

Logan had never seen anything more beautiful in his life. He damned himself for missing this the first time. Keeton looked exquisite in his pleasure.

When Keeton's muscles loosened and relaxed, Logan began to pump his fingers in and out of his mate's hole. Keeton writhed and squirmed, his legs fell open wider, and his eyes bored into Logan's.

"Now, Logan. Can't wait." Keeton palmed his cock and began

stroking it frantically.

Logan was torn. He wanted to be inside his lover when Keeton came, but he knew he needed to stretch him more. There was no rule saying that Keeton couldn't come twice, though. Smiling to himself, he inserted another finger and continued to fuck Keeton with his hand.

Keeton tugged and pulled at his prick as his balls drew tight. Logan inched back then bent to suck on Keeton's hairless sac, causing his mate to cry out, his body bucking and shaking, his hand a mere blur as he continued to jerk himself.

Logan knew his mate was close, and he wanted to see him go over the edge. Lifting his head, he looked directly into Keeton's eyes. "Come for me, baby. I want you to come now." He added a fourth finger to Keeton's clenching ass.

Keeton threw his head back and yelled as hot, pearly ropes of cum erupted from his slit. He continued to stroke himself, milking his cock until he'd coated his stomach in his seed.

"Damn, that was hot!" Keeton groaned, long and low, when Logan leaned forward to lick him clean.

He eased his fingers out of Keeton's tight channel, lubed up his cock again, and positioned the head against his fluttering entrance. He paused, not entering, looking to his lover for permission.

Keeton nodded, and amazingly, his prick began to fill again. "Fuck me, Logan."

Logan wrapped Keeton's legs around his waist and curved over his mate. Bracing one hand against the mattress beside Keeton's head, he held himself above his lover. He pushed forward slowly, breaching the first ring of muscles and not stopping until he had bottomed out.

"Sweet hell," Logan groaned. "You are so fucking tight, baby." Keeton's muscles clamped down on him, convulsing, and strangling his shaft. He groaned again. "Ease up, baby. Damn, you're going to castrate me."

"Sorry…can't," Keeton panted. "Just move."

Logan pulled out slowly, then thrust back in. He set a steady pace, already battling the urge to come.

Keeton began to relax, and Logan slid in and out of him easily, increasing his rhythm. He slipped his hand under Keeton's hips, wrapping his arm firmly around the man's lower back. Lifting his mate to him as his hips snapped forward, he pounded into his lover's welcoming body.

"Oh, oh, yes!" Keeton yelled. He moaned and whimpered, crying out over and over as he met Logan thrust for thrust.

The look of pure ecstasy on his mate's face combined with delicious sounds pouring from his open mouth, and Logan knew he wouldn't be able to hold out much longer. He released his hold around Keeton's waist and placed his hand over his lover's mouth. "Quiet," he commanded breathlessly.

Instead of having the desired effect, Keeton went wild. His cries grew in volume even as they came out muffled against Logan's palm. His small body bucked and jerked against Logan's, and he clutched at Logan's sweat-slicked shoulders.

Then suddenly, his body stilled, his inner muscles clutched around Logan's pulsing shaft, and creamy ropes of semen erupted from his cock.

He looked up at Logan dazedly and turned his head to the side, offering his neck. "Claim me," he whispered raggedly.

Logan roared loud enough to vibrate the windows, pushing into his mate as far as he could get, and followed him over the edge. He bent over his lover and sank his canines into the soft skin between Keeton's neck and shoulder. His body trembled and quaked as he emptied himself into Keeton's hungry hole, and the nectar of his blood bathed Logan's tongue.

He felt a sharp bite of a pain, followed by a gentle sucking at his shoulder, and realized Keeton had bit him. The understanding of what that meant sent Logan into a tailspin of pleasure, extending his orgasm and wrenching a muffled cry from his occupied mouth.

Once completely sated, he gently retracted his fangs from the supple flesh and slipped his spent prick from Keeton's body. He collapsed on his side and reached out blindly for his lover. Keeton came to him at once, sighing and snuggling against his chest.

"It scares me how much I love you," Logan breathed into his mate's hair. "Thank you, angel."

"I know the feeling," Keeton murmured sleepily. "I love you, Logan. Now, go to sleep." He yawned, buried his face into Logan's neck, and fell asleep instantly.

Logan tightened his hold and sighed contentedly. They had completed their mating, and no one could take Keeton from him. He would destroy anyone who tried.

Chapter Twelve

Keeton felt the sweat roll down his back and grimaced. He hated manual labor. Picking up the last box, he carried it out of his cottage to Logan's Jeep.

After he placed the box inside with the others, he turned back to his house and smiled fondly. He would miss his little place.

"Are you sure about this, baby?" Logan asked as he walked up behind him, wrapped his arms around Keeton's waist, and nuzzled against his neck.

Keeton grinned, placing his hands over Logan's arms and squeezing. "Yeah, I'm sure."

It had been two weeks since Logan claimed him. Keeton's injuries were healing at a spectacular rate now. Only four slightly raised welts remained across his torso. Logan assured him that even those would fade over the next couple of weeks.

Keeton still worried about what had attacked him, especially with the full moon fast approaching. Logan and his brothers would be running those same woods. He hoped his cousin arrived soon.

It had been three weeks since Blaise said he'd be there. There had been no other contact, and Keeton began to worry.

The Fourth of July weekend hurdled toward them as well, and he didn't look forward to that either. Logan would be working twelve-hour shifts, and while he understood Logan had an important job, he still wanted to be selfish and keep the man with him. On the upside, Logan would have three full days off after the weekend.

It could be worse, though. Xander also landed twelve-hour shifts at the firehouse, with an entire twenty-four-hour shift on the Fourth.

"I'm really glad you aren't a fireman," Keeton mumbled. He didn't know how Braxton could stand it, knowing his mate risked his life every time he went to work.

Logan just chuckled and pulled him closer. "Do you have everything?"

Keeton's lips stretched into a grin, and he nodded. He turned in Logan's embrace and wound his arms around his lover's neck. "Oh, yeah. I have everything I need."

* * * *

As soon as they turned onto the long gravel driveway that led to their house, Keeton tensed, and a sense of unease settled over him. He glanced over at Logan and noticed his mate's white-knuckled grip on the steering wheel.

Keeton sighed. The ability to feel Logan's emotions could be a big pain in the ass sometimes. Mostly, he loved it, especially when Logan was horny. With Logan's lust and desire fueling his own arousal, the sensations doubled, and already amazing sex became earth-shattering.

Times like this, however, when Logan felt angry or nervous, it could be exhausting—not to mention, frustrating as hell. Keeton knew his mate was uneasy and just a little pissed off, but he didn't know why.

He could smell things a little better since Logan had claimed him. He could pick out each of the brothers' unique scents, but he couldn't catch even a whiff of their emotions.

Keeton sighed again as he continued to look at his mate. "Logan, you might as well tell me. You know I can feel what you're feeling, and I'm going to find out anyway."

Logan echoed his sigh and closed his eyes briefly. "We have company," he grumbled without looking at him.

Keeton started to ask him to clarify his statement when they pulled up in front of the house. Everyone stood outside, huddled in a small circle, and obviously angry. Each man wore an identical expression of loathing, and their muscles seemed to vibrate with their tension. Talon yelled so loudly, Keeton could hear him through the closed windows of the SUV.

Then Boston took a threatening step forward, creating a gap between the bodies, and Keeton saw her. Mariah Bernini stood in the middle of the loosely formed circle, hands on her hips, and staring defiantly back at Talon.

Keeton flew out of his door before Logan even stopped the vehicle. He marched up to Mariah and pointed his finger in her face. "What the hell are you doing here?" he demanded.

Without warning, her hand shot out and wrapped around his throat, her fingernails digging into his flesh. "I've come to claim what is mine," she snarled at him.

Keeton heard several menacing growls, but the one directly behind him, made him tremble.

"Get your filthy hands off of him," Logan said coldly.

Mariah spun Keeton around quickly, her hand still around his throat, and his back pressed up against her breasts. "I will rip his heart out and feed it to him," she shot back just as icily.

Keeton stared into the eyes of his mate and shook his head a fraction. He did not want Logan to get involved in this. Though Mariah's nails continued to bite into his skin, he could still breathe. Besides, she was just a girl. What could she do to him?

Logan's eyes widened, and he looked horrified. "What the fuck are you?" he whispered.

Keeton didn't know what that meant, and he didn't have time to ask. Mariah's teeth sank into his skin savagely, and he screamed in pain. It didn't feel like Logan's claiming bite. This hurt like hell.

His muscles locked, and the chords in his neck strained as he continued to scream. He couldn't move, couldn't fight, his body paralyzed by the pain. Mariah didn't just bite him. She chewed at his shoulder, trying to rip the flesh away like an animal.

Then suddenly, the teeth disappeared, and the fingers around his throat released him. Keeton fell to a heap on the ground, panting and convulsing. Fire lanced through his body, burning him from the inside out. He gritted his teeth together to keep from biting his tongue as his body continued to jerk and seize.

"Blood," someone yelled. "Give him your blood."

He forced open his eyes when a familiar scent permeated the air around him. Logan leaned over him, his eyes huge and panicked. He raised his wrist to his mouth and grunted as he bit into the flesh. "Help me," he called as he forced Keeton to his back and sat on his flailing legs.

Two sets of strong hands held his body immobile. Talon held Keeton's head, and his knee pressed into one of his shoulders. Xander sat on the other side, prying Keeton's mouth open, his massive knee pressed into his other shoulder.

Logan moved his bleeding wrist over Keeton's open mouth, squeezing it with his other hand to encourage the flow. The thick, sweet-tasting liquid flowed into Keeton's mouth, and Logan stroked his throat, coaxing him to swallow it.

By the third swallow, the pain began to lessen, and Keeton's body had stopped convulsing.

"Keeton! Open your eyes, baby," Logan commanded as he lightly slapped Keeton's cheeks. It was damn annoying.

Keeton opened his mouth to tell Logan to quit it when his stomach heaved, and blood came rushing back up his esophagus. The men quickly released him, rolling him to his side as he coughed and gagged, expelling Logan's blood onto the ground.

"Keeton! Keeton!" Logan screamed. He sounded on the verge of hysteria. "Damn it, Keeton, open your fucking eyes!"

Keeton wanted to calm his mate, to tell him that everything would be okay. He was just so tired, though. He slumped heavily against the ground, and heard Logan yell his name again. It sounded faint and far away, and then…nothing.

Chapter Thirteen

"Thank you," Logan said to the stranger as he paced the living room. He had gotten Keeton cleaned up and tucked into their bed. Keeton didn't move or make a sound through the entire process. He seemed to be resting peacefully, but Logan needed him to open his eyes.

"He's going to be fine. You did well." The stranger walked up to Logan and held out a hand. "I'm Blaise Taylor, Keeton's cousin."

Logan shook the man's hand and nodded. "You look like him. I'm Logan Cartwright, Keeton's mate."

Blaise smiled, released Logan's hand, and took a seat on the sofa. He motioned for Logan to sit as well. The other members of the pack gathered around, some standing, some taking up the empty seats.

Braxton remained upstairs with Keeton. He refused to leave his friend's side. Logan understood the feeling, but he needed to know what the hell had just happened. He was extremely grateful to Braxton and promised himself to do something nice for the runt.

Looking around the room at each of his brothers, he felt his heart swell with love. "Thank you. All of you." He addressed Xander directly. "You have an incredible mate."

The brothers nodded, and Xander actually smiled. "So do you, my brother. Keeton is one of us now. I don't know what's going on, or what just happened on the front lawn, but I swear on my honor, I will do whatever I can to help you protect your mate."

"You know I've always had your back, little brother, and nothing has changed. I will defend your mate with my life," Talon said solemnly.

"He's family. Whatever you need from me, just ask," Jackson added.

"No way am I going back to being the only herbivore around here." Boston shrugged. "Besides, the little squirt has kind of grown on me."

Logan swallowed around the lump in his throat and nodded. His brothers were amazing.

"Well, you know I'm here to protect Keeton." Blaise spoke from the couch. He turned to face Xander. "I'm sorry for not announcing my presence, but there wasn't time." He stood and walked to Xander. "I ask that you allow me to stay close to my cousin, Alpha, so that I may better protect him."

Xander clapped the man on the shoulder and grinned. "You are welcome here for as long as you like. And please, call me Xander. We're all family here."

Keeton's cousin smiled and nodded in return. "Thank you, Xander."

Blaise could be the biggest prick on earth, and Logan would still feel indebted to him. Thankfully, he actually seemed to be a great guy.

Logan shuddered, remembering Mariah's face just before she bit into Keeton's shoulder. Her pupils bled out into the whites of her eyes. Her skin turned a pale gray, and bright blue veins snaked across her face. Her teeth elongated into razor-sharp daggers, and her fingernails stretched into lethal talons.

Fear paralyzed him when she sank those teeth into Keeton's flesh. Then blinding pain lanced through his shoulder and neck, stealing the breath from his lungs, and forcing him to his knees. Lava coursed through his veins, and Logan just knew his skin would melt off of his bones.

Then before he could get his shit together, a huge, black wolf came from virtually nowhere and tackled Mariah to the ground. When Logan could finally force his way through the pain and sickening heat, his mate claimed his full attention. Someone, he figured Blaise, yelled for him to give Keeton his blood. Not knowing what else to do, he complied with the directive, completely forgetting Mariah or caring what happened to her.

"Blaise, please, what the hell is going on? What was that thing?" Logan couldn't hold back the revulsion in his voice. He had dated that…that *thing*. He had been inside it.

Blaise grimaced and resumed his place on the couch. "Xander, could you please get your mate? Everyone needs to hear this, including Braxton."

He turned to Logan as soon as Xander left the room. "I have to admit, I was a little worried when Keeton told me he had mated a shifter. He's just so…fragile. You're a good mate for him, though. I can see that you love him."

"More than anything," Logan agreed devotedly.

He looked up as Braxton came racing down the stairs. Blaise had just enough time to stand before the little man launched himself into his embrace. Braxton wrapped his arms around Blaise's neck and squeezed him tightly.

"Oh, I'm so glad you're here, Blaise," he cried. "Thank you, thank you, thank you."

"You're welcome." Blaise chuckled. His head shot up, and he gently eased Braxton away from him when Xander growled deeply.

Logan sympathized with his alpha. Seeing your mate in the arms of another man—or woman—was not a pleasant experience.

"Sorry," Blaise spoke respectfully to Xander. "I haven't seen Braxton in several years. We're very close…like brothers," he added hurriedly.

Xander smiled sheepishly and shook his head. "No, I'm sorry. Braxton has told me a lot about you, and I understand. I do. My possessiveness of my mate just gets the better of me sometimes."

Braxton rolled his eyes as he went to stand beside his lover. "Overprotective idiot," he mumbled, but Logan could see the corners of his lips twitch.

"Okay, now that everyone is present and accounted for, please tell me what the fuck just happened here." Logan began to get impatient. Whatever Mariah was, she was dangerous, and she had almost killed his mate. He wanted answers.

"Mariah Bernini is a soul-sucking demon," Blaise answered flatly.

"Yeah, tell me about it." Jackson chuckled. Logan didn't really see the humor.

Blaise shook his head, unsmiling. "No, I mean literally. She is a class-four preternatural. An Arsidian Demon."

"A what demon?" Braxton sounded confused.

Join the club, Logan thought as he ran a hand through his hair. He thought he had seen everything being a preternatural himself, but demons?

"Maybe you should start at the beginning," Xander suggested.

Blaise took a deep breath. "I work for the International Council of Preternatural Justice. Simply put, I am a demon hunter. I track down demons that have been deemed a threat to the non-preter population and either bring them to The Council or execute them. I prefer the former method."

"There's a council?" Braxton asked.

"Quiet, *chulo*, let him finish," Xander admonished lightly.

"Mariah Bernini, as I said, is a class-four preternatural—the most dangerous and unstable on our registry. Arsidian Demons are the most powerful of their kind. They can take on any appearance, and are vicious and cruel."

Blaise shook his head with disgust. "They inject venom into their victims through their teeth and claws. That's what happened to Keeton both times he was attacked. It can be deadly to humans, but since Keeton is apparently part shifter," Blaise nodded toward Logan, "it probably saved his life."

Logan felt sick. He had brought this on his mate and to his family. He should have known something was very wrong when he realized

Mariah didn't give off any type of scent.

As if reading his mind, Blaise continued, "Arsidians do not give off a scent. Not from their own bodies, not their emotions, not even their blood."

"You said she was a soul-sucker. What does that mean?" Xander asked.

"Arsidians have no soul. That's what initially alerted me. Keeton told me that Mariah lacked the core of her aura. Arsidians survive by killing their victims and absorbing their souls."

"That's really gross," Braxton stated in disgust.

"Okay, but why didn't she just kill me? I mean, I dated her for more than a month. And why pretend to be pregnant?" Logan felt so confused, his head started to throb.

"You are cursed shifters, yes?" Blaise's tone held no judgment.

"Yes."

"The magic surrounding you is very powerful. I can feel it now, even though you are all in your human forms. Especially you," Blaise motioned to Logan, "and you," he pointed to Talon. "As twins, your magic is almost doubled, more so when you are together. If an Arsidian was to mate with you and produce one of your offspring…" Blaise trailed off, shaking his head. "They would be unstoppable."

"So, that's why she was pawing at me after Logan dumped her?" Talon asked.

"Yes and no. I think she planned to mate each of you. Arsidian females are able to produce as many as a dozen offspring at one time. They can mate several different males when they go into heat. They can also carry the offspring of each male at the same time."

"Holy shit," Boston breathed, speaking for the first time. "So, you think she was planning to mate all of us?"

Blaise nodded. "Yes, I think so. She would have specifically wanted Logan and Talon, but I think she would have tried to seduce each of you before her mating heat had cycled."

"So, she's in heat right now?" Logan asked, clarity coming to him swiftly. "That's why she lied. She wanted me to stick around long enough to actually impregnate her when she began her cycle."

Blaise nodded again. "Correct."

"So, is she in heat now?" Jackson repeated Logan's question.

"Yes."

"And how long does that last?"

"Until the setting of the next full moon." Blaise turned to Logan. "You are very lucky, friend. Her cycle probably started just days after you ended your relationship with her."

"So, how do we stop her?" Xander asked.

And wasn't that the million-dollar question.

Chapter Fourteen

Keeton came awake with a cry, his limbs flailing as he fought off an invisible attacker. Heavy, muscular arms wrapped around him, causing him to panic and freeze in terror.

"Shh. Easy, angel. I'm here. I'm right here. I've got you, baby."

Keeton's tensed muscles began to relax as Logan's soothing voice washed over him. He melted into his lover's embrace, clutching at the front of Logan's shirt. "She bit me," he huffed indignantly.

"I know. I'm so sorry, Keeton." Logan eased him away and looked directly into his eyes. His jaw clenched, and a fierce determination blazed across the harsh lines of his face. "I will never let her near you again. I swear to you."

"I know you would protect me with your life." Keeton wanted there to be no doubt in Logan's mind that he understood exactly how much the man loved him. "I would much rather it didn't come to that though."

Logan crushed him close again. "How are you feeling, baby?" he whispered into Keeton's hair.

"Better than I did the last time something attacked me." Keeton took an inventory of his body. His neck felt a little tender where he'd been bitten, but at least there wasn't a gaping hole. All in all, he felt okay. "Is it because you gave me your blood?"

"Yes," Logan answered, still holding Keeton to him. "Only because you are my *sienota*, though. If I tried to give my blood to anyone else, even one of my brothers, it would make them very sick."

Keeton just nodded against Logan's chest. "What is she, Logan?" He hadn't seen Mariah since she had been standing behind him.

Judging by the look he had witnessed on Logan's face, it must have been horrific, though.

"I think I can answer that," came a voice from the doorway.

Keeton pulled away from Logan and beamed at the newcomer. He knew that voice. "Blaise!"

Blaise grinned at him as he moved into the room and settled down on the side of the bed. "Hello, little cousin."

Keeton threw himself at Blaise, knocking the wind from his cousin. After only a second, he jerked back and whipped his head around to stare at his mate. Logan growled warningly, his eyes locked on Blaise's throat.

"Logan?" Keeton asked.

Blaise, however, just chuckled as he stood from the bed. He looked at Keeton and shook his head. "You and Braxton are going to get me killed."

Oh! His very protective and possessive mate was having issues with him hugging another man.

Keeton rolled his eyes and allowed himself to be pulled back into Logan's arms. "Behave," he whispered to his mate.

Logan sighed and nuzzled against Keeton's neck. "Sorry, baby."

He shivered when Logan's lips caressed the sensitive skin on his throat. His body arched toward his mate, and his cock went rock hard in less than a second. He needed the feel of his lover's hard body, his hands, and his mouth caressing him to replace the memories of that bitch touching him.

Keeton glanced up at his cousin when he heard Blaise groan. He knew Blaise could smell his arousal, but he didn't much care at the moment. The only thing Keeton had on his mind was getting his lover naked and on his back.

"You can watch if you want," Keeton smirked at his cousin, "but I intend to have my sexy mate's enormous cock buried deep in my ass in the next three seconds." Keeton shrugged. "Your choice."

Blaise's eyes widened, and he held up his hands. "I'll pass."

"Good answer," Keeton mumbled as he watched him retreat from the room.

"Would you have really let him watch?" Logan asked, slipping Keeton's shirt over his head. He rose from the bed and pulled Keeton to his feet.

"Not a chance," Keeton stated vehemently. "This gorgeous ass is mine." He grabbed a handful of Logan's left cheek to reiterate his claim. "It's fun to watch him get flustered, though."

Logan swept him into his arms and carried him from the room. "Where are you taking me?" Keeton grumbled. He hadn't been joking about having Logan buried balls deep in his ass.

"Shower," Logan grunted.

Keeton's heart raced, and his breath caught in his throat. Oh yeah, the shower had definite potential. "I think our next house should have private bathrooms in all of the bedrooms. This communal stuff blows."

Logan's steps faltered, and he looked down at Keeton in surprise. "Our next house?"

"Yeah, Braxton told me about that silly curse you guys think you have. He said that you have to move around a lot so people don't get wise about you always being MIA on the full moon, or because sometimes people see you when you're out hunting."

"Braxton has a big mouth," Logan groused. "He's right, though. We do move around a lot. We've only been here for a couple of years however, and we have our own land to run and hunt on now."

Logan set him on his feet inside the bathroom and reached around him to turn on the water in the shower. "Our biggest threat," he continued, "is from other shifters and preters that know about our difference. We've been hunted for as long as anyone can remember. That's usually why we have to end up moving."

Keeton flipped the button on his jeans and slid them off his hips. He watched, licking his lips, as Logan stripped out of his clothes as well.

"How many times have you had to move?" Keeton had never had such a casual conversation in the nude before. He didn't think he'd ever had *any* kind of conversation in the nude before. It felt very domestic.

Logan motioned for him to enter the shower before stepping in behind him. "Only six times in the last sixteen years." He shrugged as he began soaping Keeton's body. "Not so bad."

His hands moved over Keeton's skin, leaving a trail of heat behind them. Closing his eyes, he moaned when Logan gently cupped his balls and began washing the delicate sac. His cock, which had gone limp during their conversation, began to fill and swell again.

His eyes flew open, and his body jolted when Logan wrapped his slippery hand around Keeton's shaft and stroked lightly.

"There are those beautiful eyes," Logan cooed to him. He leaned forward and captured Keeton's mouth in a scorching kiss.

The tingle began in Keeton's lips and quickly spread throughout his body. He moaned into Logan's mouth as his hips began to thrust in and out of his loose grasp. He whimpered in frustration. "Logan, please."

"Please what, baby?" Logan's voice was thick and gravelly. His own erection jutted out from his groin, rubbing itself against Keeton's stomach.

"Please, sir. I want you, Logan."

Logan groaned, lining his cock up with Keeton's, and wrapped his big hand around them both. Keeton added his own hand, thrusting more quickly in and out of their combined grip. Logan gave a little twist of his wrist, adding a wonderful friction around the head of Keeton's prick.

Placing the thumb of his other hand against the slit in Logan's dick, Keeton began rubbing quick circles along the very tip of the head.

Logan went crazy. His body jerked, and his muscles tensed. He thrust erratically, and with such force, that Keeton had to release his hold on their weeping cocks and grab Logan's shoulder to keep from falling over. Logan's grip became almost painful as he kept up the quick strokes with his hand.

Then he wrapped a hand in Keeton's hair and tilted his head roughly to the side. He bent over him and sank his teeth into Keeton's neck, right over where Mariah had bitten him.

Keeton shuddered and groaned loudly as his hips snapped forward, and he sprayed Logan's hand and wrist with his seed.

When he came back down to earth, he immediately realized that his mate needed to come. Logan leaned back against the shower wall, jerking his prick roughly, his eyes closed, and his breathing ragged.

Something was wrong, though. Logan's expression looked more pain than pleasure. The head of his cock flushed a deep purple, his balls drawn tight and close to his body. His eyes snapped open, and he looked at Keeton pleadingly.

Keeton almost went to his knees, but he wanted to claim his mate again. He couldn't do that with Logan's cock in his mouth. So, he stepped in between Logan's spread thighs and batted away his lover's hand, replacing it with his own.

He stroked his mate quickly, adding a little twist around the underside of the head as Logan had done to him. He used his other hand to lay his palm flat against the tip, over the slit, right where his thumb had been. Keeton moved his hand in quick, small, concise circles, applying just the right amount of pressure.

Logan yelled, throwing his head back and arching his hips up into Keeton's grasp.

"That's it, baby. Feels good, huh? You like what I'm doing to you?" He seduced with his words as he continued to use his hands to push Logan closer and closer to the edge. Leaning forward, he swirled his tongue around one of Logan's nipples, before sucking it into his mouth.

"Oh fuck. Oh, oh, oh. Keeton!"

When he had Logan bucking and thrashing, mindless with

pleasure, he inched up further and bit into his smooth pectoral.

Logan roared loud enough to shake the entire room. Long, creamy ropes of hot semen rocketed from his exploding cock, coating Keeton's hand, wrist, and stomach.

Keeton stroked a few more times, milking Logan's orgasm, demanding his mate give him everything he had to offer.

Logan slumped against the tiles, his body limp, and a very satisfied look on his face. Keeton smiled tenderly at his mate and reached for the soap to clean his lover.

Wrapping his hand around the back of Keeton's neck, Logan gently massaged the muscles with his fingers. He pulled him close, pressing their lips together, kissing him slowly and adoringly. Keeton melted right there on the spot.

"Love you so much," Logan whispered against his mouth.

"I know." He smiled up at his mate.

"Smart-ass." Logan chuckled and swatted Keeton's ass.

They finished cleaning themselves, dried off quickly, and raced back down the hall to their bedroom. They dove under the blankets and wrapped around each other in a tangle of arms and legs.

Keeton sighed happily as he rested his head against Logan's chest, letting the steady beat of his mate's heart lull him to sleep.

"Hey, Logan?"

"Hmm?" Logan's voice was thick and drowsy.

"I love you, too," he whispered.

"I know, baby. I know."

Chapter Fifteen

When Keeton woke again, he found himself alone, Logan's side of the bed cold, and the room dark. He could hear voices floating up to him from downstairs and decided to go investigate.

Feeling mischievous, he rummaged through his drawer, pulling out a pair of rainbow-colored, spandex boy shorts. He could already picture Logan's face.

His stomach snarled angrily, reminding him that he hadn't eaten anything since breakfast. He hoped Logan had cooked. None of the other brothers could boil water without burning it.

He found he was in luck as he walked into the kitchen. His mate stood over the stove, stirring something that smelled like heaven and made Keeton's mouth water.

Braxton's loud laughter reached him immediately, followed by Blaise's spluttering. "Holy shit, Keeton!"

Logan glanced over his shoulder and dropped the spoon to the floor. The poor guy looked in danger of passing out. "Keeton!"

Keeton giggled, turning around and shaking his spandex-covered ass. "You like?" He popped his hips one way and then the other, the writing across his ass blinking red and gold.

"*Naughty* indeed," Braxton purred. "Yummy!"

Logan growled as he marched across the kitchen.

"Oops. Gotta go," Keeton said, smiling brightly. He waved cheerily to his best friend and his cousin before turning and darting out of the room.

Once in his room, he quickly pulled on one of Logan's T-shirts. He briefly considered skipping the pants, but decided he'd probably pushed Logan far enough for the time being. Grabbing a pair of his own sweatpants, he tugged them on and hurried back to the kitchen.

Logan turned and glared at him as he shuffled into the room. "If you're done showing off your assets, would you like to eat?"

Keeton groaned and rubbed his stomach. "I'd eat the damn spoon, I'm so hungry."

Logan's face softened, and he chuckled. "Almost finished," he said, turning back to the boiling pot on the stove. "You eat cheese, right?"

"Yeah," Keeton answered, smiling. It was sweet that Logan always tried to accommodate his diet.

Turning again, Logan cocked his head to the side as he stared at him. "You don't eat animals, but you wear them?"

Huh? "Huh?"

"Those white leather pants you have in our closet," he elucidated.

Keeton shook his head and rolled his eyes. "Those are just really well-made faux-leather. No animals were harmed in the making of them." Keeton took a seat at the table. "Where is everyone?"

"Talon, Boston, and Xander are at work. Jackson went for a run. Blaise and Braxton left after your little performance." Logan narrowed his eyes at that. "They're going down to Carpe Noctem." He sat a steaming plate in front of Keeton as he spoke.

Keeton picked up his fork and shoved a bite of the pasta in his mouth. It tasted incredible, and he moaned like a porn star in appreciation.

"Spinach and three cheese tortellini in roasted tomato Alfredo sauce with sautéed asparagus." Logan puffed out his chest proudly. He sat beside Keeton and dug into his own plate.

"Could we go meet them?" Keeton asked uncertainly, not looking at his mate. Other than the short trip to his cottage to pack his things, he hadn't been out of the house since he arrived. He was going stir-crazy.

"Uh...well..." Logan trailed off.

Keeton tried to keep the disappointment out of his voice. "That's okay. I just thought we could go out since it's your last night before you start your twelve-hour shifts." He knew Logan was only trying to keep him safe, but he didn't know how much more he could take.

Logan sighed, and Keeton could feel the emotions warring inside his lover. "Would you like that, angel?" Logan asked finally.

Keeton bit his lip and nodded. Inside, however, he was doing the conga.

"Okay." Logan nodded absently as if deciding something. "We can go, but I want you to stick close to me. I want your promise, Keeton."

Keeton jumped up from his chair and dived into Logan's lap. He wrapped his arms around his lover's neck and kissed him breathless. "Thank you," he panted when he broke the kiss.

He expected Logan to smile or say something sarcastic. He didn't expect Logan to growl and push him back on the table. His lover was instantly on him, licking and sucking at Keeton's lips as plates and glasses shattered to the floor.

"I've been too easy on you, angel." Logan pulled Keeton's shirt over his head and twisted it around his wrists. "Maybe you have forgotten who's in charge here."

Keeton shook his head quickly. He reached out, searching Logan's emotions, relieved to find only lust and a fierce sense of possessiveness.

He bit his lip to stop his grin. He knew this game. He knew his role, how to play it, and the way the scene would end. He knew exactly what Logan needed from him, and was happy to give it.

"You've been a very naughty boy, Keeton," Logan rasped as he slipped Keeton's sweats off of his body. He smacked the blinking decal on Keeton's underwear before sliding them off as well. "Very naughty, indeed."

Keeton trembled, and his mouth went dry. He'd only seen this side of Logan once before, and he couldn't wait for a repeat performance. He found something comforting in Logan telling him what to do and how to do it. It left little room for mistakes.

Logan seemed to be waiting for a reply. "I'm sorry, sir."

Keeton's voice came out barely more than a ragged whisper. His cock was hard and aching, twitching with anticipation. He didn't know what his lover was talking about, or what infraction he had committed.

Resuming his seat, Logan pushed Keeton's legs back until his heels rested on the table. "What are you sorry for, angel?" Then he leaned forward and swiped his tongue across Keeton's quivering hole.

Keeton groaned loudly. His body jerked, and his legs fell open in a wanton display of surrender. He was putty in Logan's hand—or mouth—or whatever.

A sharp smack to his outer thigh made him cry out. "I d-don't know. I'm sorry for whatever I did to displease you."

Logan laved Keeton's hairless sac, then flattened his tongue, licking a wet line from his anus to the tip of his leaking cock. "Not good enough," Logan said as he sat back. "You need to understand what you did wrong so that you do not repeat the same mistakes."

He wrapped his hand around Keeton's shaft and began stroking him hard and fast. Keeton arched up into his lover's tight grasp, his orgasm building.

Then Logan's hand disappeared.

Keeton groaned in frustration. He was so close. The pressure in his balls built until they felt in danger of exploding.

"Now, why are you sorry, Keeton?" Logan drew tiny circles with his forefinger on the back of Keeton's thigh.

Logan wanted him to think? Keeton could barely remember his last name. "Please, tell me."

"If you don't know what you've done, then how can I be positive that you are really repentant?" Logan sounded almost amused, the bastard. "What are the rules? You do remember the rules we talked about, yes?"

Keeton wracked his brain for any tiny spark of remembrance. Clearly, Logan wouldn't allow him to come until he felt satisfied with Keeton's answer. "Never allow anyone else to touch me in an intimate way!" he sang out triumphantly.

"Very good," Logan breathed across Keeton's opening. He lapped and sucked, driving Keeton out of his mind, before backing off again. Keeton growled as he let his head fall to the table with a thud.

"Now, have you broken that rule, angel?"

"No!" Keeton denied heatedly. "Never!"

"Hmm." Logan trailed his fingers lightly along the underside of Keeton's balls. "So, you did this all on your own then?"

Oh, fuck! Keeton didn't know how Logan had found out about that, but he knew he was in deep shit. "It wasn't intimate, Logan!" Keeton raised up just enough to look into his mate's eyes. He didn't mind playing this game with Logan, but he wanted there to be no doubt about what had happened with Jackson.

"I just needed Jackson's help. I swear I would never be unfaithful to you." He hoped his lover could hear the sincerity in his voice, feel the emotions that he pushed at him.

Logan's eyes softened, and he nodded. "I know, angel. It's okay." He stood and leaned over Keeton, placing a sweet and tender kiss against his lips. "You still need to be punished, though. And I want your word that it will never happen again."

Keeton nodded. "I promise."

Logan rolled him onto his stomach, pushing his knees under him, and pulling his ass back to hang over the edge of the table. "I think one swat for each time you allowed Jackson to touch you."

Keeton's heart kicked into high gear, and he began to pant. "It was only the once," he managed.

"Oh, no, baby. How many strips did he use to make these balls so nice and pretty for me?"

Keeton gulped. "Uh…four."

Logan caressed each of Keeton's rounded cheeks as he spoke.

"Let's just make it a rounded ten, shall we?" His hands disappeared for a split second before a stinging swat landed on Keeton's ass.

He cried out and tried to wiggle forward, but Logan clamped down on his thighs and held him in place. "Oh, no, you don't." He licked Keeton's ass, soothing the burn from his hand. "Now." Logan's voice was deep and commanding and sent a jolt of electricity straight to Keeton's cock. "Do. Not. Move."

Keeton bit his lip to keep from moaning like a slut and nodded. "Yes, sir."

Logan continued to deliver his punishment, alternating sides with each smack to his heated flesh. Keeton held still by sheer force of will. His straining dick leaked so copiously, a small pool of pre-cum formed on the table beneath him.

"One more, angel. Your ass is so fucking gorgeous right now—all red and scorching hot for me. Are you ready for the last one?" Logan's voice sounded shaky, and Keeton knew his lover was not as in control as he wanted to appear.

"Yes, sir," Keeton answered firmly. He cried out again when Logan's hand landed on his ass, just barely holding back his orgasm. He hadn't been told not to come, but instinctively knew he shouldn't.

"You did so well, baby. I think you deserve a reward."

Logan parted Keeton's cheeks, and cool air rushed over his twitching hole. Wet, slippery warmth quickly replaced the cool breeze, and Keeton shivered and moaned.

Logan licked, sucked, and prodded his entrance, reducing Keeton to a writhing pile of goo on the table. He took him to the edge several times before backing off, just to do it all over again.

Then Logan's tongue pushed inside his slippery hole, and Keeton almost choked. No one had ever done anything like this to him before. It felt so good, and he never wanted it to stop.

A finger slipped inside his hole beside Logan's tongue, and Keeton forgot his orders not to move. He rocked back and forth, fucking himself on Logan's finger, needing just a little more to push him over the edge and into euphoria.

Logan's face disappeared from between Keeton's spread globes, but he continued to work his finger in and out of Keeton's ass. "No coming. No moving." Logan paused, and when he spoke again, Keeton could hear the smirk in his voice. "And not a sound. Understood?"

Keeton nodded reluctantly. His dick throbbed so hard, it would probably break off when he finally found his release.

* * * *

Logan smiled as he felt Keeton shudder beneath his palm. He didn't exactly understand why his little man got off on Logan denying him to voice his pleasure, but he had no problem giving in to his mate's unspoken desires.

Smoothing his hand down Keeton's sweat-slicked back, he admired the flush of his lover's skin. Keeton was the most beautiful thing he had ever seen, and he found something very erotic about having his mate spread open, completely naked for him, while he remained fully dressed.

Logan smiled again. He really liked that idea. Pushing his sweats down, just enough for his straining cock to pop free of its confinement, he tucked the waistband just under his balls.

Damn, they needed lube. He was much too big to penetrate his mate with only his saliva to ease the way. Adding another finger to Keeton's clenching hole, he darted his eyes around the kitchen for something, anything, he could use as slick.

Logan looked back at his lover to find Keeton smiling at him over his shoulder. "There is a bottle of lube in the junk drawer."

He didn't know why the hell there was lube in the kitchen, or how Keeton knew where to find it. He didn't really give a shit either. Pulling his fingers from Keeton's ass, he hurried to the drawer beside the sink, and returned in less than a second.

He poured a generous amount into his palm, slicked his throbbing shaft, then slipped three fingers into Keeton's hungry ass. His mate's body seemed to suck his fingers right in, drawing a deep groan from Logan's chest.

He hoped Keeton was ready because he couldn't wait any longer. He had to be inside his mate, and he needed it right fucking now. Logan pumped his fingers a few more times before slipping them free and lining up the head of his cock.

"No moving, no coming, and no noise," he reminded his lover. Keeton nodded and gasped, but said nothing. "Good boy."

Logan pushed forward in one long stroke, seating himself to the root inside his mate. He groaned loudly, and his fingers dug into Keeton's hips in a bruising grip. "Damn, you are always so fucking tight."

He began thrusting in and out of his lover in quick, hard jabs. Some part of his brain worried he was being too rough with his mate, but he couldn't stop. He would just have to trust that Keeton would tell him if he did anything to hurt him.

Leaning over Keeton, bracing both hands on the table on either side of his lover, he felt his orgasm rush toward him. The tightening and burning of his lower belly, the tingle in his balls, the flash burn across his skin, heralded one hell of a climax to this little interlude.

"Come, baby. I want you to come, and I want you to scream my fucking name. I want everyone in the tri-county area to know who you belong to." Logan increased his pace, slamming into Keeton's hot ass. "Come. Now!" he grunted.

Keeton's body jerked once, twice, then froze as his muscles tensed, and his inner walls squeezed Logan's cock. Logan yelled, growled, snarled, and hissed as his orgasm blasted from his body, coating the silky lining of Keeton's clenching tunnel.

Keeton threw his head back and screamed Logan's name so loudly, he thought his eardrums would bleed.

Chapter Sixteen

Logan sucked in a breath through his gritted teeth. When Keeton had come down the stairs in a pair of painted-on, ripped jeans that showed more skin than they covered, he should have known it would be a long night.

Shifting in his seat, the bulge behind his zipper making him uncomfortable, he took a long swallow of his beer. Logan watched the object of his desire twirl and gyrate out on the dance floor. He'd have to talk to his brother about having Keeton banned from the place without an escort.

Keeton had gelled his hair in its customary spikes, but had combed his bangs down to fall to one side of his forehead. With the navy blue eyeliner, the sheer, light blue, sleeveless shirt, and the sexy pout of his lips, he looked lethal.

Logan's eyes narrowed, and his jaw clenched as some muscle-bound asshole in leather pants walked up behind his mate and wrapped his gorilla arms around Keeton's waist.

Keeton quickly danced out of the embrace, twirling to shake his finger at the man. He pointed in Logan's direction, and Logan saw him mouth the word, "Taken." Then he looked directly at Logan and crooked his finger. Twice.

Logan didn't dance. He shook his head and smiled at the pout on Keeton's lips. Keeton shrugged, wrapped one arm around Braxton's waist, and began a slow grind.

Logan was out of his seat and moving before his brain registered the intent to do so. He marched out onto the dance floor and right up to tower over his mate. "What the hell are you doing?" he roared over the pounding of the bass.

"Dancing," Keeton yelled back with a wicked grin.

Logan grabbed him around the waist, hauled him over his shoulder, and strode off of the dance floor.

"What the hell was that for?" Keeton demanded angrily when Logan sat him on his feet beside their table.

"Don't start with me," he warned.

Keeton crossed his arms and huffed as he sat down in one of the chairs. Logan thought he looked adorable—and hot as hell.

"C'mere, baby."

Keeton hesitated for just a moment before smiling widely and jumping into Logan's lap. He straddled his thighs, rocking his groin against Logan's belly.

"Are you having fun, angel?"

"Yeah." Keeton nodded. "I needed this. It feels good to get out there and move with the music. Why won't you dance with me?"

Logan chuckled and kissed his lover's protruding lower lip. "I don't dance. I told you that."

Keeton looked disappointed for a moment then shrugged. "Oh, well, I have Braxton to dance with." He smiled mischievously, his eyes twinkling.

Logan laughed again and shook his head. "Not gonna work, Keeton."

He just winked and jumped up from Logan's lap. "I'm going to the little boys' room."

Logan started to rise. "I'll go with you."

Keeton pushed him back down in his chair and glared. "I am perfectly capable of going tinkle on my own. Just sit."

Logan nodded, but he didn't like it. Looking out onto the dance floor, he found Blaise watching Keeton walk toward the restrooms at the back of the club. He glanced over at Logan, pointed at his chest, then jerked his thumb toward Keeton.

Logan nodded. Hell, yes, he wanted Blaise to follow Keeton.

He had explained the situation to his mate on the way to the club, telling him everything Blaise had said about Arsidian Demons, Mariah being in heat, and how dangerous she could be.

Keeton still didn't seem to be taking any of it seriously.

Standing from his chair, he headed toward the exit. He needed air. Blaise would keep an eye on Keeton until he came back, but just in case, he asked Talon to do the same as he passed him on the way out. His twin nodded and began scanning the room immediately.

Logan stepped out into the muggy night and walked around the side of the building to the dark alley. Everything was falling apart, and he hadn't even had five minutes to digest it.

Leaning against the rough bricks, he closed his eyes and breathed in deeply through his nose. His head pounded, his stomach twisted, and the muscles in his back were so tight and knotted, he felt like they would snap his spine.

He stood that way for a long time, but when he opened his eyes, Keeton stood in front of him, wearing nothing but a pair of black, bikini briefs and an adoring smile.

"What the hell are you doing? Where's Blaise? Where the fuck are your clothes?" Logan yelled in shock. What on earth was his lover doing?

Keeton pushed himself against Logan, molding their bodies together, humming happily. "I thought you could use a little stress relief."

Though all about relieving some stress, he wouldn't fuck Keeton in some grimy alley as if the man was a cheap prostitute. "Keeton…"

Keeton would hear none of it. He rubbed his palm over Logan's growing erection and began licking at his throat. "Come on, Logan. I know you want me."

He couldn't deny it. Everything about his little mate turned him on—his soft skin, the way he moved, and his perfectly heart-shaped ass.

Above all, he loved the way his mate tasted. Logan wrapped his arms around Keeton, and crushed their mouths together, running his tongue over Keeton's lips, begging to taste the warm sweetness inside.

Keeton moaned, and Logan forced his tongue through the parted lips.

And froze.

He tasted nothing. Logan inhaled deeply, looking for the strawberries and sugarcane scent of his mate, and again, finding nothing. He suddenly recalled Blaise's warning that Arsidian Demons could take on any form.

Keeton could be a bit flamboyant, but he didn't act like a skank. Logan should have realized something was wrong immediately, but he'd let his dick do his thinking, and now he was fucked.

He shoved roughly at the Keeton impostor and snarled. The smile on the fake Keeton's lips turned malicious, evil, and Logan hoped he never saw it on his angel's face again.

Then the body in front of him began to vibrate so quickly it became nothing more than a blurry shadow. When the shaking stopped, Mariah stood before him with her hands on her hips, wearing only the bikini briefs, her breasts fully exposed.

She hissed at him. "You will be mine, Moonlighter. Make no mistake."

"Never," Logan spat.

"I seek retribution, and you will help me claim it."

Then she threw her head back on her shoulders and let out an ungodly shriek. It sounded like nothing Logan had ever heard before, and it scared the shit out of him. He watched as her skin began to turn that sickly gray color and her pupils bled out to bathe her eyes in onyx.

"Oh, shit." Logan inched his way to the corner of the building, his eyes never leaving Mariah's screaming figure.

Before he could take his second step, her head snapped up and her intense gaze bore into him. She opened her mouth, showing off her razor-sharp teeth, and licked her purple lips. "Yum," she rasped. The sound of her voice left Logan feeling cold down to his soul.

"Logan! Where are you? Logan!"

Mariah's focus whipped to the mouth of the alley, and she grinned wickedly. Logan's heart seized, and terror clogged his airway. *Not Keeton!*

He launched himself at the demon, not daring to take the time to shift. Logan was quick, but Mariah was quicker. Her fingers elongated, resembling twigs from some twisted old tree, straight out of a horror movie. Her fingernails lengthened into four-inch claws, and she swiped at Logan as he dove toward her.

Mariah's talons slashed across Logan's chest from shoulder to shoulder, the claw from her forefinger slicing across the side of his throat. She snarled at him before turning and sprinting down the alley.

Logan fell to his knees, his hand clutched over the bleeding wound on his neck. The pain was intense. He felt like his chest was on fire, and his wounds continued to bleed freely. Panting and groaning, he struggled against the sickening heat that threatened to drag him under.

It took only seconds for him to realize that he fought a losing battle.

* * * *

Keeton stood on the sidewalk in front of the club, hands on his hips, looking one way and then the other along the street. Talon told him that Logan had gone outside to get some air. Where the hell was he?

Sharp, excruciating pain hit Keeton in the chest, causing him to stumble backward. He clutched at his chest, wheezing breathlessly, as the pain tore through him.

Logan.

A soft groan from the side of the building drew Keeton's

attention. He shuffled toward the corner of the club, and sniffed the air, using his newfound abilities to search out his wayward mate.

His olfactory senses weren't nearly as developed as the rest of the pack, and he still had a hard time sorting out different smells, but he'd know Logan's scent anywhere. It hit him with such force that he gasped.

"Logan?" Keeton really did not want to go into that alley if he didn't have to. He had watched enough of Logan's gory slasher movies to know that nothing good ever came from entering dark alleys.

Another soft groan floated to him in reply. He took a deep breath to steady his resolve and stepped around the side of the building.

"Oh, God," he gasped.

He rushed over to his fallen mate, slowly rolling Logan to his back. There was blood everywhere. Keeton frantically felt around his lover's neck for a pulse. His fingers slipped over the gaping gash on Logan's throat, and he felt the tears well up in his eyes.

Why wasn't Logan healing? True, the cuts were deep, but they should have at least stopped bleeding. If Keeton didn't do something soon, his mate would not survive.

"Logan." He slapped at his lover's cheeks. When he received no response, Keeton began to panic. "Logan!" he screamed. "Don't you dare die on me, you son of a bitch! That would really ruin my fucking day."

The tears began to roll over his cheeks in earnest. "Logan, please," he sobbed.

He knew he needed to go find help, but he couldn't just leave his mate to bleed out in some disgusting alley. So, he did the only thing he could think of. He threw his head back and yelled as loudly as he could.

"Blaise! Talon! Braxton! Someone! Anyone!" Keeton continued to scream over and over until he heard footsteps thundering down the sidewalk, hurrying toward him.

Talon rounded the corner first, Blaise quick on his heels. Braxton came next, followed by Boston, who quickly grabbed the smaller man and held him back. Braxton kicked and flailed, screaming random threats and imaginative obscenities at the brother.

"Xander will kill me if I let anything happen to you. Stay put!" Boston ordered.

Talon and Blaise dropped to their knees beside Logan and quickly started assessing his injuries. "He needs blood," Blaise said as he looked up at Keeton.

"But, I'm not a shifter. Not really. One of you give it to him."

"It doesn't matter," Blaise spoke quietly, obviously trying to soothe him. "You're his mate. It has to be you. It will help." Blaise grabbed Keeton's shoulders and shook him roughly. "Trust me."

Keeton nodded numbly. He wasn't so sure his cousin hadn't lost his mind, but he was willing to try anything to save his mate. He grabbed a piece of glass from a broken beer bottle off the ground and, before he could chicken out, sliced it across his forearm.

Blaise groaned. "I think we could have found something a little cleaner than that." He indicated the bloody piece of glass in Keeton's hand.

"No time." Keeton shook his head and hurried to kneel over his mate as blood dripped from his arm. Talon held his brother's mouth open, and Keeton let the thick red liquid pour into his lover's mouth.

Please, God, let this work.

When he had gotten as much blood into his mate as he could, he wiped his arm on his shirt and grabbed Logan's face in both hands. "Logan Edward Cartwright, you open your eyes right now!"

Logan's eyelids fluttered, and he moaned weakly. "That's it, love. Come on. Open your eyes." Keeton kept up his flow of encouragements even as the tears continued to fall from his eyes.

"Let's get him home." Talon spoke for the first time since entering the alley. "Boston, go tell Seth someone else is going to have to close up," he called over his shoulder, not looking away from his wounded brother.

Talon and Blaise lifted Logan and carried him through the parking lot to Logan's SUV. They eased him into the backseat, and Talon dug through Logan's pockets to find the keys and tossed them at Blaise.

"Get them home. We'll be there soon."

Keeton slid into the backseat and managed to get Logan's head positioned in his lap. He stroked his lover's hair away from his handsome face. "Stay with me, love. Stay with me."

Chapter Seventeen

"Start talking, Blaise," Keeton demanded. "I want to know what happened to Logan. Where the hell are my parents? What are you even doing here? And how do we stop that bitch?"

Keeton was exhausted. He'd been up all night worrying about his mate. Blaise was quick to assure him that shifters healed swiftly. He also reminded Keeton that if Logan felt the urge to keel over, Keeton would know it and wouldn't be feeling up to being so annoying.

Blaise held up his hands. "Calm down, Keeton. Your mate needs to rest so that he can heal himself. You know he can feel your emotions, and he won't be able to rest easily if he can feel how worked up you are."

Keeton nodded and took several deep breaths. "I know, and I'm sorry. I also know that this isn't your fault." He wrung his hands together as he gazed up at his cousin from his position on the love seat. "Just tell me what's going on. Please."

Blaise sighed and sat down beside him. "Logan told you what Mariah Bernini is, correct?" He waited for Keeton's nod before continuing. "And he explained why she is so intent to have him, as well as the rest of the pack?"

Again, Keeton nodded. "She wants to breed with them. She can carry each of their babies at the same time, and she will feed off the souls of those babies until they are born. That's just creepy, dude."

Blaise grinned, but without much humor. "You have no idea, little cousin. Shifters of the Moonlight Breed are surrounded by such powerful magic that if she were to succeed, she would be nearly invincible."

"Moonlight Breed?" Keeton cocked his head to the side.

"That's what The Council calls shifters like Logan. Those that have white pelts when they shift," he elaborated. "Hasn't he explained it to you?"

Keeton shook his head. Braxton had told him a little about it, but apparently, he was missing something.

"Moonlighters are very rare. Only one per generation is born to each colony. Well, two in the case of twins like Logan and Talon. Other preters can sense their power even when they're in human form. When they shift, however, the magic around them is so powerful it will drive anyone close to them to insanity almost instantly."

"So, I won't ever be able to see Logan shift?" Keeton frowned. Logan had promised, and he knew his mate would never jeopardize his safety that way.

"No, you're fine. Mates are the exception to the rule, as well as other Moonlighters. You can see Logan shift, just not anyone else in the pack."

"But, Logan said he's a snow leopard. Isn't that a species of leopards? They live in the Himalayas. It's not like being a white tiger or white stag like Xander or Boston."

"It's different with shifters," Boston explained as he entered the room. "There is a wide range of species that we can shift into, but none of those include species with white coats. No polar bears, snow owls, snow leopards, or anything like that." He shrugged as he plopped down on the sofa.

Keeton shrugged as well and turned back to his cousin. "So, if these little baby demons are going to be Arsida-whatevers, how is their slut-whore mother going to feed on their souls? I thought they didn't have one."

"If an Arsidian female mates with a male not of her kind, the offspring will carry the soul of the father. The mother will feed on their souls, and whatever magic they possess, until there is nothing left. That's why a female will try to mate with as many men, as many times as possible, during her heat. The more offspring she carries, the longer she can feed from them."

"But wouldn't that kill the little ankle biters?" Keeton scrunched his eyebrows in confusion.

"A person can live without their soul. Arsidians are proof of that."

"Okay, but you said they had to kill to ingest the soul of their victim."

Blaise shook his head. "No, they do not have to kill to gain another's soul. They merely enjoy it." His eyebrows scrunched together and the corners of his mouth turned down. "Although, death would be preferable."

"Well, I don't know what it's like to live without a soul, but I think it would be better than dead."

Shaking his head again, Blaise's frown deepened. "I don't know about living without a soul, but once an Arsidian Demon gains possession of your soul, they own you. They can control your mind, your body, make you do horrible things."

Keeton gaped at his cousin. "Get out of town!"

"The more powerful a preter's magic, the longer an Arsidian can control them. Once the soul has been consumed, the link is broken."

Keeton shuddered in revulsion. They definitely needed to change the subject. "Okay, so where are my parents?"

"They're chasing dragons," Blaise said without a hint of sarcasm.

"What the hell? What do you mean? My parents are chasing ancient mythological creatures?" Keeton's brain hurt.

"Since Anna went off to college last year, they have taken a position with The Council. They are currently in Indonesia on a peacekeeping mission with a colony of Komodo Dragon shifters."

"Are you kidding me?" Keeton yelped. "And nobody thought it might be a good idea to tell me?" He clutched his head in both hands. "This is insane."

"Everything will be fine, Keeton. Your parents aren't Hunters like

I am. Think of them more as ambassadors. They are completely safe, and they should be home in a couple of weeks."

"I'm going to check on Logan. When I come back, someone better be making some damn sense. You," he jabbed his finger at Boston, "go make us some breakfast that doesn't involve a rotting animal carcass. And you." Keeton pointed his finger in Blaise's face. Then he dropped his hand and shook his head. "I can't even look at you."

Standing, he stalked over to the staircase. "Stupid shifters. Crazy ex-girlfriend demons. My cousin thinks he's some modern-day Van Helsing, and my parents are off playing tiddlywinks with fucking dragons," he mumbled to himself as he made his way up the stairs.

He didn't miss the snorts of amusement from the living room below.

* * * *

Logan was awake, sitting against the headboard, and poking at the angry red welts on his chest when Keeton walked into the room. The wounds had closed, but Blaise said it would be another couple of weeks before they would completely heal.

Rushing over to the bed, he grabbed Logan's hand and tugged it away. "Would you stop that? Do you know how many germs and bacteria are on your hands?"

Logan just looked at him and grinned. "Hey, angel."

Keeton rolled his eyes, but he couldn't help but smile in return. "Hi back. How are you feeling?"

"Better now that you're here," Logan crooned as he pulled Keeton to him and kissed his lips.

Keeton felt the tears prickle the corner of his eyes, and he swallowed around the lump in his throat. Sniffling, he pulled back from his mate and shook his head.

"You know that if you die, so do I?" Keeton raised his eyebrows. "I'm already way behind on the character panels that Braxton wants, so dying would be quite inconvenient for me right now. Maybe you could try to stay out of trouble, hmm?"

Logan chuckled and reached for him again. "I promise, baby." Pulling Keeton into his lap, he devoured his mouth in a kiss that Keeton felt right down to his toes.

When they finally broke apart, Keeton was surprised to find his lover frowning. "We have to stop her. Do you finally realize how serious this is? I need you to stay out of trouble as well. My heart can't take the strain of worrying about you all the time."

Keeton nodded thoughtfully. "There is a soul-sucking she-demon in heat that is determined to breed with not only my mate, but the rest of my family as well. Yeah, I think I got a handle on the current situation."

"Keeton," Logan warned. "She is dangerous. Please, understand this."

"I do," he answered seriously. "I'm not going to sit around and feel sorry for myself, though. It's just not who I am."

"Okay," Logan relented. "I get that. Just be careful. Please. And you realize that you're under house arrest until Mariah is caught, right?"

"Yeah, I kind of figured you were gonna go all wicked stepmother and lock me in the tower." He snorted and rolled his eyes.

"It'll just be for a little while." Easing Keeton from his lap, Logan stood and pulled on a pair of sweats, then motioned for Keeton to come to him. "We need to talk to Blaise."

"Fine," he said following Logan down the stairs. "I can't imagine why you would want to, though. He's an idiot."

"I heard that, asshole!" Blaise called from the kitchen.

Keeton covered his mouth to stifle his snicker, but quickly gave up the effort when Blaise came barreling into the room. Keeton shrieked and jumped behind Logan, latching on to his mate's shoulders and trying to climb the man's back like a spider monkey.

Logan shrugged him off easily and spun out of Keeton's reach.

"Oh, no, you don't. You started this." Grabbing Keeton around his upper arms, he held him immobile.

Keeton struggled against Logan's hold, even kicking his feet off the ground, but Logan still held him easily, suspended in midair.

"He's all yours."

Keeton looked up and over his shoulder at his lover. Logan looked at Blaise, grinning like a Cheshire cat. Whipping back around to stare at his cousin with wide eyes, Keeton started shaking his head frantically and redoubled his efforts to free himself.

"No. No, Blaise, please. Come on, man, you know you're my favorite cousin. I was just joking, really."

Blaise smiled impishly as he slowly stalked forward.

"Logan!" Keeton pleaded. "Come on, love. You know you don't want to do this. What happened to protecting me and all that stuff?"

Then Blaise pounced.

Keeton screamed and tried to curl into a ball, but Logan lowered him to the floor and pinned him as Blaise tickled his ribs, his stomach, even under his arms. Struggling to breathe through the shrieks and giggles, Keeton couldn't believe his cousin and mate had ganged up on him like this.

Only when Keeton was sure that he had started to turn blue from lack of oxygen did they release him. He lay on the floor, limp and defeated. "Not. Fair," he managed to gasp as he fought to regain his breath. "I hate you both."

"No, you don't. You *lurrrv* us," Blaise sang.

Keeton lifted himself up on his elbows and stared at his cousin. "You did not just say 'lurv.' Even I'm not that gay."

Blaise just laughed and flipped him off.

"So, how do we stop her?" Logan said out of nowhere.

The atmosphere of the room sobered instantly. Keeton sat up and quickly scrambled into Logan's lap. If they had to talk about unpleasant things, at least he could be comfortable.

Logan stood, easily cradling Keeton in his arms, and sat on the sofa. He positioned Keeton more securely in his lap and wrapped his big, powerful arms around him. Keeton sighed serenely and burrowed into his lover's embrace.

He loved having Logan wrapped around him like this. It was like a warm cocoon of peace and safety, and he felt loved and cherished, protected and cared for. Nothing could touch him when he was in Logan's arms.

Logan leaned down and brushed his lips softly across Keeton's brow. Tilting his head up, he captured his mate's searching lips, moaning like a champ.

"Not to break up the little gagfest you two have going on, but we need to come up with a plan," Blaise admonished them. He sat on the floor, looking slightly annoyed.

"Fine," Keeton huffed after breaking the kiss. "So, what is your brilliant plan, Oh Great Demon Slayer?"

"Keeton," Logan and Blaise both growled at the same time.

"We are running out of time," Blaise continued. "The mating heat will end with the setting of the full moon. In five days," he expanded. "She will be getting desperate, which does not bode well for us."

"Why can't she just go bang some other shifter?" Keeton wondered out loud.

"Arsidian females choose the male or males they intend to breed with before the start of their mating heat. It's like a sport for them, a game." Blaise shook his head. "Technically, she could mate with anyone, but she won't. She's too invested in her conquest now."

"Okay, but why did she choose us?" Logan asked. "I know what you said about the whole magic thing, but there has to be more to it than that."

"As I explained to Keeton, if she were to allow you to live, she could control you once she has absorbed your essence. She would be unstoppable."

"You keep saying that." Keeton sat forward in Logan's lap. "What does that even mean? It's not like she's going to take over the world."

"Not the world," Blaise agreed. "I did a little digging after Logan's attack and found records in The Council database indicating that Mariah Bernini has been exiled from her legion."

"Wow, she's even too crazy for a pack of demons," Keeton said around a snicker.

His cousin glared at him, but otherwise didn't comment.

"She said something about wanting retribution, and I was going to help her get it." Logan tilted his head to the side in question.

"It makes sense," Blaise conceded. "If she were to succeed in breeding with each of you, as well as absorbing your souls, *and* have the ability to control you, she could easily wipe out her entire legion."

"I don't like the idea of her sucking down my mate's soul like an appetizer, but what's wrong with her taking out a bunch of demons? You said they were vicious. I thought that would be a good thing." Keeton struggled to keep up with the conversation, but his head swam with information overload.

Shaking his head, Blaise took a deep breath before he answered. "By eliminating her legion, the lands they control would fall under Open Territory laws. Hunting lands are scarce, and the Old South Legion resides over some prime real estate in Alabama. If the lands were no longer occupied, it would be a full out preternatural war."

"And if she doesn't mate before the end of her cycle. What happens then?" Logan asked, changing the subject. Keeton kissed his jaw in gratitude. He didn't want to talk about war, death, or slurping down souls like banana smoothies.

"She will be weakened and ultimately more desperate. She will need to feed on many souls to replenish her strength and power."

"So, we just have to make it through the next five days and then strike while she's weakened?" Logan frowned. "That seems too simple."

"Because it is. Even in a weakened condition, she will still be stronger than any one of us."

Keeton let his mind drift as Logan and Blaise continued to talk strategy. He really did need to catch up on the story panels for *Quest*. He had done some sketches for Braxton, but he needed to get started on the storyboard for the demon characters.

He didn't miss the irony. The demons he and Braxton had created, however, looked like creepy little children. They were strong and formidable, with only one weakness. Neither he nor Braxton had come up with that weakness yet, but every villain had to have one so that the hero could extort it and vanquish the evil.

"I have to go get ready for work." Logan's words interrupted Keeton's internal monologue.

With everything that had been going on, he had totally forgotten it was Friday, and the beginning of the July Fourth weekend. Logan had to be at work at noon, and he wouldn't get home until well after midnight. His mate would be out in the night with a crazy demon on the loose.

Keeton extracted himself from Logan's hold and made his way up the stairs and to his room without saying a word to anyone. He had reached his breaking point and couldn't form words around the lump in his throat, even if he had something to say. Everything was crashing down around him, and he felt helpless to stop it.

Climbing into bed, he wrapped himself around his pillow and cried.

Chapter Eighteen

Logan rose from the couch and made to follow Keeton. He could feel the depression and the hopelessness flowing from his mate. It made his heart ache and his stomach clench. He needed Keeton more than he needed his next breath, but maybe he had been wrong to bring him into their world.

"Let him go." Blaise stood in front of him, blocking his way. "He needs to work through this for himself."

Logan shook his head. Something was terribly wrong with Keeton. His light had dimmed. His usual buoyancy and charismatic charm were fading.

"Move," he growled.

"Logan, listen. Keeton can be a bit of a drama queen. He'll be fine, though. Just let him have his tantrum, and he'll get over it."

Logan snarled. The man obviously knew nothing about his cousin. Keeton wasn't throwing a tantrum. He was scared for himself and for the people he loved. He was miserable because he felt useless, powerless, and helpless. Logan could feel all of those emotions pouring into him from his lover.

"Get the fuck out of my way. You know nothing about him."

Blaise looked shocked for a moment before anger darkened his features. Nodding curtly, he sidestepped to let Logan pass by him.

Logan ran up the stairs, taking them two at a time, and paused outside the closed door to his and Keeton's bedroom. He turned the handle, surprised to find it locked.

"Keeton, open the door," he said softly. "Please, don't shut me out."

No movement sounded from the bedroom. Logan rested his forehead against the cool wood and closed his eyes. "Come on, angel, open the door. We don't even have to talk. I just want to hold you," he coaxed. "Please, just let me hold you."

Finally, there were sounds of movement and the metallic click as the lock disengaged. He waited a moment, then eased open the door when it remained closed.

Keeton lay in the middle of the bed with his face buried in a pillow. His small body shook, but no sounds escaped him. Walking to the bed and sliding in beside his mate, he pulled Keeton to him without a word.

Keeton clung to him, sniffing and sobbing against his chest. Logan had never heard anything more heartbreaking. "I'm so sorry, angel," he whispered into Keeton's hair.

Keeton shook his head slightly. "It's not your fault. I'm just being a big wimp."

Recalling Blaise's words, Logan gently extracted himself from Keeton's hold and tilted his face up to look into his eyes. "You have every right to your feelings. Anyone would be upset and afraid. These," Logan brushed away Keeton's tears with his fingertips, "don't make me think any less of you."

Keeton gave him a watery smile and sniffled. "I bet I look awful." He rubbed under his eyes with his fingertips, frowning when they came away wet and smudged. "My eyeliner is all smeared." He sniffed loudly. "And my nose is running like a horse in labor."

Wrinkling his nose at the mental image of a horse running while in labor, Logan opened his mouth to question the strange analogy.

Before he could respond, however, there was a soft knock on the door. Blaise stood in the open doorway with his head hung, looking guilty and ashamed.

"Hey," he said weakly, still staring at his knees. Then he looked up and focused his gaze on Keeton. "I'm sorry, man."

Keeton didn't ask why. He didn't say anything. He just turned to

Blaise, nodded, and opened his arms. Smiling sheepishly, Blaise hurried to the bed to throw his arms around his cousin. "We're going to figure this out, Keeton. I promise. I won't let anything happen to you."

Logan grinned and rose from the bed to finish getting ready for work. He knew that Blaise and Keeton were close, and he was glad they could work things out.

"And I promise I won't let anything happen to Logan or Braxton, or anyone else," Blaise continued. "I'm sorry that I treat you like a kid sometimes. I just worry about you, ya know?"

Logan looked over to see Keeton smiling. It looked good on him, and Logan hadn't seen it near enough of over the last few days.

"We're good, Blaise. Don't worry. I'll be fine. All this," Keeton waved his hands vaguely around the room, "it just gets a little overwhelming sometimes." He shot Logan a glance full of love and tenderness. "But it's all worth it."

Logan swallowed around the sudden tightening of his throat and turned away from Keeton so his lover wouldn't see the moisture in his eyes. All he had ever wanted was for someone to look at him the way Keeton did—as if he had hung the stars and roped the moon.

Logan knew he loved Keeton, but until that moment, he had not realized how much he needed him. Keeton had wormed his way into his heart, and there was no turning back.

"I have to get going." He spoke with his back still to the other men in the room. "I'll be home a little after one, so don't wait up for me."

"I'll talk to you later," he heard Blaise whisper.

Tiny arms wrapped around his waist, and Keeton pressed his face into Logan's back. "I will always wait up for you."

Logan turned in his lover's embrace and crushed Keeton to his chest. He held him tightly, gently rocking side to side, and breathed in the warm, rich scent of his mate. Then he eased away and cradled Keeton's face with both hands.

"Stay inside the house. Please, I'm begging you. No matter what, do not leave this house. Jackson and Blaise are here, and they will keep you safe. Promise me, baby."

Keeton rolled his eyes but grinned sweetly. "I promise…on one condition."

Logan just raised a brow in question. He would give Keeton anything he wanted if it meant he would stay inside and keep himself safe.

"Please, be careful out there." Keeton's voice shook with emotion. "Take care of yourself and watch your back. I expect you to come home to me the same as how you left."

Logan leaned forward and brushed his lips against Keeton's forehead. "You got it," he whispered. Then he claimed his lover's lips in a kiss full of promise, pouring all of his love and devotion into the mating of their lips.

Long moments later, Keeton jerked away, gasping for air. "Go, before I tie you up and molest you."

Logan chuckled, stole another quick kiss, and hurried out of the room. He had never been on the receiving end of a rope or handcuffs, but the idea of letting Keeton restrain him had his cock perking up in interest. Maybe they would have to explore the idea sometime.

* * * *

"Okay, so what's the plan?" Keeton paced the living room as he spoke with Blaise and Braxton. Jackson was in the kitchen, as usual, making a late-night snack of spaghetti with meatballs.

"I honestly don't know, little cousin." Blaise shook his head as he stared down at his knees. "No one has ever successfully taken an Arsidian Demon alive before. Hell, there are only two cases where some lucky bastard was able to kill one."

Keeton huffed and fell into one of the overstuffed recliners. "This is bullshit. You are freaking shifters for pity's sake. What makes this bitch so special that you can't even kill her?"

"For one, she's fast, much faster than any one of us. She's also stronger than any of us. She may look petite and fragile, but she could rip your throat out with two fingers before you could even blink."

"Okay, so she's faster and stronger than any one of you." Braxton spoke up from where he sat on the floor. "What if you all teamed up against her? And wouldn't one of the pack shifting in front of her make her go all fruit loop?"

"Theoretically, yes," Blaise answered. "But she would kill them before they even had a chance to finish their change. As for us teaming up against her, well…"

"Well?" Keeton asked when Blaise didn't continue.

"I hadn't really thought of it, to be honest. It would probably be our best shot, but we'll have to come up with a plan, beginning with a way to lure her to where we want her."

Before anyone could speak again, Keeton's cell phone began to ring. He snatched it up and frowned when he didn't recognize the number on the caller ID. "Hello?"

"Keeton," Logan spoke tightly, "Xander has been hurt. They're taking him to Community North Hospital. I need you and Braxton to meet me there."

Keeton glanced at Braxton and then quickly away. He closed his eyes, and his heart bled for his best friend. "How bad?"

"Pretty bad. They're not sure if he's going to make it. You guys need to hurry, Keeton."

"Okay, we're on our way. I love you, Logan."

"Love you, too, Keeton." Then the line went dead.

Keeton slid his phone into his pocket and slowly turned to face Braxton. "We need to go, Brax. Xander's been hurt. Logan says we need to hurry." He spoke quietly, each word costing him more than anyone could know.

He expected Braxton to jump up and become an instant whirlwind of motion. At the very least, he thought Braxton would ask what had happened. Keeton didn't know what to think when Braxton just snorted and rolled his eyes.

"Xander isn't hurt."

"Honey, that was Logan on the phone. He said we need to meet him at the hospital."

"You aren't going anywhere," Blaise stated firmly. "Either of you."

Keeton rounded on his cousin. "Blaise, you don't understand. Logan said they didn't think Xander was going to make it. We have to go!" He was shouting by the time he had finished. "What is wrong with everyone?"

"Xander isn't hurt," Braxton repeated. "I would know. I'd be able to feel it. Just the same as you would if Logan was hurt." He grabbed his own cell phone from the coffee table and dialed.

After a short pause, Braxton smiled and spoke into the phone. "Hey, big guy, how's work going?" Another brief pause, and he chuckled softly before speaking again. "I'm sure that can be arranged. Hurry home, and I'll have everything ready when you get here." His eyes went misty, and he smiled tenderly. "Love you, too. I'll be waiting."

Keeton put his hands on his hips and glared first at Braxton, then Blaise, and for good measure, he glared at Jackson as the brother walked into the room. "What the fuck is going on?"

"Well, I thought it would be obvious." Blaise smirked. "That wasn't Logan on the phone. If I had to guess, I'd say it was Mariah."

"I know Logan's voice, and that was definitely him on the phone," Keeton argued.

"Was it his number?" Jackson spoke around a mouthful of pasta.

"Well, no, but I just assumed that it was the hospital's number or something."

"The voice may have sounded like Logan, but did he really sound like himself?" Braxton asked.

"Well, he sounded a little strained, but since I thought Xander was hurt, I figured that was pretty reasonable." Keeton cocked his head to the side as he thought. "He kept calling me Keeton."

"Well, that is your name." Jackson looked confused.

"No. I mean, yes that is my name. Logan rarely ever calls me by my name, though. It's always angel or baby." Keeton closed his eyes and groaned. "I'm such an idiot."

"You're not. I'm sure I would have freaked, too, if Xander called and told me Logan was hurt." Braxton came over and hugged Keeton. "You just have a really big heart, and sometimes it clouds your judgment. Why don't you call Logan? His shift is almost over anyway."

Keeton glanced at the clock above the fireplace, surprised to see it was already after midnight. It seemed his plan to preoccupy his time by working on character panels and storyboards for *Quest* had worked. He'd barely had time to miss or worry about Logan all day.

Nodding, he pulled his phone from his pocket again, hit the speed dial for Logan's number, held the phone to his ear, and waited. He didn't even realize he'd been holding his breath until it all came out in a great whoosh when Logan answered on the third ring.

"Baby? Are you okay? What's wrong?" Logan fired off immediately.

"I'm fine," Keeton hurried to reassure his mate. "Everything is okay. I got a phone call a few minutes ago that kind of shook me up."

"What phone call? Who called? What happened, angel?"

Keeton smiled to himself. Now that he wasn't panicking because he thought Xander had been hurt, the differences between Logan, and Mariah pretending to be Logan, were exceedingly obvious. "Don't worry, love. I'll tell you all about it when you get home. Which is soon, right? I miss you."

He heard Logan sigh over the phone. "I'm leaving now. I'll be home as quickly as I can get there. Do not leave the house, and do not let Blaise out of your sight. Understood?"

"Yes, sir," Keeton whispered.

Logan groaned. "Oh, you are trouble. I think maybe someone needs a good spanking when I get home."

Keeton felt his cock twitch at the thought of Logan spanking his ass. He bit back a moan and quickly turned his back to the other men in the room. "Hurry."

Logan chuckled and hung up.

Keeton smiled, sliding his phone back into his pocket, and turned to see Jackson and Blaise staring at him with identical grins on their faces. "You heard all of that, didn't you?"

"Every word." Blaise smirked wickedly.

"What? What's going on?" Braxton demanded.

Keeton just shook his head ruefully. *Stupid shifters.*

Chapter Nineteen

Saturday flew by without incident. There were no strange calls or she-bitch demons showing up unannounced. No one tried to infiltrate the fortress. No one tried to breed with or kill anyone. No one even showed up to sell them a vacuum cleaner.

Keeton sighed as he kicked off of the porch and set the swing in motion. Logan had once again made him promise not to leave the house for any reason, and he couldn't help but feel like a teenager, grounded for staying out past curfew.

"House arrest blows," Keeton mumbled to himself as he continued to swing. He wasn't accustomed to sitting home and doing nothing.

"I am not a fucking child, and this is stupid." Hauling himself up from the swing, he marched determinedly across the porch. Just as he made it down the front steps, headlights turned off of the main road and onto the long, gravel drive.

He sighed. That would be the warden, coming home from his shift. Well, Logan could just kiss his ass. He was tired of being on lockdown, and he was breaking out.

Keeton hurried to his car and jumped in, thankful that they lived out in the boonies and he could leave the keys in the ignition. Though not exactly dressed to go clubbing in a black tank top, faded jeans, and flip flops, it would have to do.

He started down the drive slowly, wanting Logan to see him leaving. Childish and petty, yes, but he couldn't help it. He had been caged for too long.

The white Jeep travelling toward him veered suddenly and came at him head-on. Keeton shrieked as he slammed on the brakes and tugged the wheel sharply to the right. His little car skidded along the gravel, did a half turn, and came to an abrupt stop when the back end collided with the piped fence.

The Jeep idled in the middle of the drive, and Keeton saw Logan open the door and step out. Though too dark to see the expression on his face, Keeton could feel the anger radiating from his mate. *Yeah, well tough shit.* Logan wasn't the only one pissed.

Keeton threw open the door, propelled himself out of the car, and strode straight up to his peeved lover. "What the fuck was that for?"

"Where the hell do you think you're going?" Logan countered. "I told you not to leave the house!"

"I'm not a fucking child, nor am I a prisoner. I'm not even a fucking princess you can lock inside the highest tower." Keeton had moved past the point of yelling and right on to screeching, but there was no stopping now. "And even if I were, you are supposed to be the knight that comes and rescues me. Not the troll that put me there in the first place!"

"This is ridiculous." Keeton yelped when Logan lifted him off his feet without warning and threw him over one heavily muscled shoulder. "You are not going anywhere, so just shut up, put on your big girl panties, and deal with it, Your Highness."

That's it. Keeton completely lost his shit. He began kicking and screaming, beating on Logan's rock-hard back with his fists. "Put me down, asshole! I can go anywhere I want. I swear, I'm going to kick your ass!"

He yelped again when he felt himself flying through the air and abruptly deposited on the front porch. "Oh ho, going to kick my ass, huh?" Logan smirked. "You and what army, little man?"

Keeton didn't know what came over him. He had never been more pissed off at anyone in his life. He glared up at his mate for a split second before his fist shot out, seemingly of its own accord, and connected squarely with Logan's nose.

"Oww!" He had never hit anyone before. It hurt like hell. Cradling his hand to his chest, he glared at his lover again. It was all Logan's fault anyway.

The glare quickly slid off his face, and he slapped his left hand over his mouth. Blood ran profusely from Logan's nose, dribbling over his mouth and down his chin to soak his shirt. "Oh crap," Keeton breathed through his fingers.

Logan pulled his shirt off and mopped the blood from his face. He gingerly fingered his battered nose before turning a menacing glare on Keeton. "You broke my nose, you little shit!"

"Oh crap," Keeton whispered again before darting off the porch and around the side of the house. He didn't get more than a dozen steps before Logan tackled him from behind. Keeton squeezed his eyes shut and waited for the bone-jarring impact.

It never came. Instead, he landed on top of Logan, his back to Logan's chest. Angry, and with every right, Logan still protected him.

All at once, Keeton felt ashamed of his juvenile behavior. The rational part of him knew that Logan wasn't trying to make his life miserable. He only did what he could to make sure Keeton even had a life.

And rather than being grateful for a mate that loved him enough to go to any lengths to protect him, Keeton acted like a spoiled, immature brat because he couldn't go play with his friends.

He didn't know what to say. "Sorry that I punched you in the face" seemed kind of inadequate. So, he said nothing and rested his head on Logan's shoulder.

* * * *

Logan felt the tension ease out of his mate, and he wrapped his arms tighter around Keeton's torso. He didn't know what had possessed the man to haul off and punch him in the nose, but he imagined it had to be something big. Keeton just wasn't a fighter.

Damn if his angel didn't have a mean right hook, though. Logan knew the bleeding had stopped, and he could feel his nose mending, but it still ached. He figured it would be tender for a day or two.

Fighting back had never even crossed his mind. He'd sworn to protect Keeton from anything—including himself. The adrenaline still pumped through his body, searching desperately for an outlet. Without the anticipation of a good brawl to calm his racing pulse, his body directed the energy into new pursuits.

He caressed his hands down Keeton's stomach, pushing up the hem of his tank top to get better access to all of that smooth, creamy skin. Tracing his tongue along the gentle curve of his mate's neck, he nipped lightly at his earlobe, as his cock jerked and swelled.

"I missed you," Keeton whispered, his body shivering. "Sorry I punched you in the face." He craned his neck to the side to give Logan better access.

Snorting softly against the sweet-smelling skin of Keeton's throat, Logan teased, "You hit like a girl." He slid one hands into the waistband of Keeton's baggy jeans and groaned deeply when his fingers encountered nothing more than flesh. "Want you, baby."

"Mmm, yes," Keeton purred. His back arched, and his ass rubbed against Logan's straining erection. Reaching over his head, he wound his fingers in Logan's hair and turned to press a hungry kiss to his mouth.

"Lift up a little." Keeton complied instantly, planting his feet on the ground and thrusting his pelvis into the air. Logan quickly unbuttoned his own pants and slid the zipper down in one fluid motion. He pushed his pants down his hips, and hissed when his naked flesh connected with the cold, dew-covered ground.

His hiss became a quiet moan when his mate's hot skin pressed against him, trapping his throbbing cock between their bodies. Keeton wiggled and gyrated, kicking his jeans off his feet, and grinding his ass against Logan's groin. Slowly, deliberately, he began rotating his hips as he slid his hands up the inside of his thighs.

Logan grasped Keeton's hips, stilling his movements. If his little mate didn't stop, Logan was going to blow his load before they even got started. "Put your legs on the outside of mine."

When Keeton did as asked, Logan bent his knees and used them to press his mate's legs even wider. He licked and nibbled along his lover's neck and shoulder, using one hand to palm Keeton's pulsing shaft, and moving the other to Keeton's mouth.

Keeton parted his lips and sucked those fingers right in, moaning as he did. "That's it, angel," Logan crooned. "Get them good and wet."

He removed his fingers from Keeton's mouth, reached under one of his spread thighs, and pressed his slick digits to his mate's puckered hole. Circling the ring of muscles, he coated the entrance with saliva before pressing in with both fingers.

Keeton groaned, and his entire body jerked. "Are you okay, baby? Talk to me."

"Don't stop," he whimpered as he rocked up and down, fucking himself on Logan's fingers.

Logan grinned against Keeton's shoulder. "I have no intentions of stopping until you're screaming my name." He sawed his fingers in and out of his mate, twisting and scissoring as much as their positions would allow.

Keeton's moans increased in length and volume, and Logan knew he hovered on the edge. Removing his fingers from Keeton's body, he wrapped his hand tightly around the base of his cock. "Uh-uh, no coming until I say."

Keeton groaned, pinching the inside of Logan's arm. "Then stop being a damn control freak and fuck me already."

"No lube," Logan growled in frustration. "We need lube, or you won't be walking right for a while."

Keeton wiggled until he rolled off of Logan's body and reached for his jeans. Digging around in the pocket, he pulled out an individual packet of lube and tossed it at him. "Problem solved."

His joy that his lover had come prepared didn't last long before jealousy reared its head. Keeton had been on his way out when Logan ran him off the road. So, of course, he hadn't been anticipating their little rendezvous. This meant that Keeton had other intentions for that little foil envelope. Which meant...

Logan sat up quickly, reached out, and grabbed Keeton by his shoulders. He pulled his mate to him roughly until their noses were almost touching. "Do you mind telling me why you were leaving the house with a packet of lube in your pocket?" he snarled.

"What?" Keeton yelped. He struggled to free himself from Logan's grip. "Logan, stop it! You're hurting me!"

"Do you have a condom in those jeans as well, or did you intend to just go bareback in a stall of some bathroom? Sure, you're immune to diseases now that I've claimed you, but most guys would insist on a condom."

"What the hell are you talking about?" Keeton demanded as he tried in vain to pry Logan's fingers from his arms.

"I'm talking about worrying myself sick over trying to keep you safe, and you repaying me by going out to get your rocks off with the first guy that drops his pants!" Logan hissed.

Keeton went completely still and stared at him with wide eyes. Not the response Logan had expected. Nor did he expect Keeton's expression to turn to a glare of pure hatred.

"You gave me that lube pack two weeks ago and told me to keep it on me at all times. Maybe you have a guilty conscience. Something you want to tell me?" His voice was so calm, so low, it scared the hell out of Logan.

He did remember giving Keeton that little envelope of lube. It was just after he had claimed Keeton for the first time, and he'd been having difficulty keeping his hands off of his mate. He'd wanted to make sure they always had the necessary supplies.

He let go of his mate and jerked his hands away. The look Keeton gave him was filled with fire, and not the kind that meant he was about to get lucky either. "Oh, baby, I'm sorry. I'm so sorry."

"Fuck you, Logan." Keeton grabbed his jeans and began to pull them on. "This is bullshit. You keep me locked up in this house like it's a fucking prison. You never want to go out or take me anywhere." He buttoned his jeans, shaking his head slowly. "Now you accuse me of being unfaithful."

He didn't know what to say. Everything Keeton spat at him was true. He reached out for his lover, but Keeton dodged his advances.

"You can't just hug me and kiss me and pretend everything is okay. Nothing is okay. Everything is going to hell." He looked Logan right in the eye as he slowly backed away. "And that's exactly where you can go as well."

Logan knelt, rooted to the ground, watching his mate turn and walk around the side of the house. Had Keeton just dumped him? Well, he had news for his little man. Logan wouldn't let him go without a fight. They were mated, and not even death would separate them.

He just had to figure out how to fix everything he'd broken between them.

Chapter Twenty

"Hey, where the hell have you been?" Blaise demanded as Keeton stepped through the front door.

"Piss off, asshole." He pushed his way past his cousin and hurried up the stairs to his room.

He'd no more made it through the door when Braxton stepped in behind him. "Did you have a fight with Logan?"

"Something like that," Keeton mumbled. "He keeps me under house arrest. I can't even go out and get my hair done." He tugged at his blond locks. "Then to cap it off, he accuses me of cheating on him. Or, well, planning to anyway."

Braxton sighed. "Surely, you have realized by now that the men in this house tend to be a little…extreme. Your cousin included. Tell me what happened."

Keeton gave Braxton an abbreviated version of the events that had unfolded on the side lawn. "He's the one that gave me the lube!" he yelled in conclusion.

"Idiots, all of them." Braxton sighed again. "How would you have reacted if your positions were reversed?"

"That's not the point." Keeton pouted. "He gave it to me!"

"Yes, I get that, but what if you had forgotten…in the heat of the moment…that you had given Logan a packet of lube? Not to mention that you come home to find him headed off to who knows where."

"I'd probably go apeshit," Keeton conceded.

"Logan asked me a question one time, when I was all pissy with Xander for his over-protectiveness." Braxton took Keeton's hand and smiled just a little. "What would you do to keep him safe?"

Immediate and sure, Keeton responded, "Anything."

Braxton's smile widened. "That's what I said. Logan doesn't mean to treat you like a child. He's trying to keep you safe the only way he knows how."

Keeton closed his eyes and swallowed down the sudden burn in his throat.

"You're connected to your mate. I know you can feel him. Tell me what he's feeling right now," Braxton cajoled.

Keeton took a deep breath, cleared his mind, and reached out to his mate. Lost in his own depression, he had been blocking Logan's emotions for several days. He wasn't even sure how he'd done it, and part of him feared he wouldn't be able to bridge the gap between them.

Gasping, moisture pooled in his eyes as Logan's anguish and regret pushed at him like a battering ram. A heavy blanket of despair fell over him, dropping Keeton to his knees. He leaned over, rested his forehead against the plush carpet, and let the tears fall down his face.

Braxton knelt beside him, placed a warm hand against his back, and rubbed gently. "It's not too late, honey. You and Logan have something very special. Don't let that go over something as silly as pride."

Sitting up, Keeton swiped away the tears with the back of his hand as he faced his friend. "When did you get so smart and rational?"

"When I fell in love," Braxton answered seriously.

Keeton placed a gentle kiss on Braxton's cheek. "Thank you. You are the greatest."

Braxton nodded. "Ditto. Now, go find your man." He rose to his feet and reached out to help Keeton up. "Just don't wander too far or Blaise will have a coronary."

"No promises." Keeton winked. He hugged his best friend briefly before hurrying out of the room in search of his mate.

* * * *

Keeton found Logan in the backyard, kneeling in the grass and staring up at the moon. He approached his mate slowly and stood behind him, laying a hand on Logan's bare shoulder.

"Your aura looks like shit." Logan's aura still had its ice blue core, but the surrounding rings were gloomy shades of gray and brown.

"It's almost the full moon," Logan commented without looking away from the lunar orb.

"I know," Keeton answered softly. He hadn't yet experienced a full moon with his mate, but the thought made him a little sad. He couldn't be near the rest of the pack when they shifted. He understood the reason, but he still felt disappointed that he would have to sit at home while Logan and his brothers ran and played in the woods.

At least he would have Braxton for company. Braxton had been through three full moons since he had mated Xander. Keeton idly wondered how the full moon would affect him now that he'd been *activated,* so to speak.

"I'm sorry, angel," Logan whispered, interrupting his thoughts. His head dropped, his chin resting on his chest. "I was an asshole, and I had no right to treat you that way. The thought of anyone else touching you just makes me insane, and I can't think straight."

Moving to kneel in front of his mate, Keeton placed a hand on Logan's thigh. "Look at me."

Though slow to raise his head, when he did, Keeton could see the moon reflected in the shining of his lover's eyes. He caressed Logan's cheek softly. "I love you. Nothing is going to change that. You couldn't get rid of me if you tried. I have a temper, and I say things I don't mean when I'm upset. But, you can't just give up so easily."

Pulling Keeton to him, Logan crushed their mouths together in a kiss that was both hungry and possessive. He trailed his lips down Keeton's neck, sucking and biting. "Oh, make no mistake, my angel. I will never let you go without a fight."

Keeton would have jumped for joy if his body hadn't been melting under the assault from Logan's mouth. Hot and strong, Logan's hands slipped under the hem of Keeton's tank top to map the skin across his lower back.

He shivered and writhed, his body going from zero to overdrive in a span of seconds. His skin on fire, his blood boiling, he knew he would die if he didn't have Logan, and soon. "Please," he whispered. He had no idea what he begged for, but knew only his mate could give it to him.

"Tell me what you want, baby. Anything you want, I'll give it to you." Logan's hands moved around to grip Keeton's hips, pulling him into his lap.

He whipped Keeton's shirt over his head and latched on to a nipple. Logan licked, sucked, and nibbled until it pebbled and Keeton's cock ached for the same attention.

He moaned and rocked in Logan's lap, pushing his throbbing erection against the bulge in Logan's pants. Winding his fingers in Logan's hair, he arched into his mate's mouth as primal need bubbled up inside him.

Pulling Logan's head back, Keeton stared into his eyes for several seconds. "Make love to me, Logan. Claim me, right here, by the light of the moon."

* * * *

His chest constricted as he looked into the beautiful Caribbean blue eyes of his mate. Logan's entire world revolved around the man in his arms, and he was powerless against him. He knew they were mated, his brothers knew they were mated, but Logan needed something more. He wanted everyone to know Keeton belonged to him, and only him.

"I love you more than all the stars in the sky, Keeton Taylor. I promise I won't ever let you down, or fail you. I will always put you first." He placed a gentle kiss against his lover's lips. "Marry me."

"Oh," Keeton gasped. His eyes filled with tears, and he wrapped his arms around Logan's neck, squeezing him tightly.

Logan figured that was answer enough, but he needed to hear the words. "Baby, please say something."

"Yes, yes, yes," Keeton whispered brokenly into Logan's neck. He sat up and smiled so beautifully, Logan felt like his heart would beat out of his chest with happiness. "How could it ever be anything but yes? I love you, Logan Cartwright, and I would be honored to be your husband."

Logan pulled Keeton close and kissed him deeply, slowly maneuvering them until Keeton lay on his back, Logan hovering over him. He trailed kisses down Keeton's neck, his chest, down his stomach to the waistband of his jeans.

"I grabbed more lube," Keeton panted as he squirmed. "Right pocket."

Logan dipped his fingers into his lover's pocket and extracted a half-empty bottle of lube. He sat it on the ground beside Keeton's hip and went to work divesting him of his pants.

Keeton's hard cock sprang free to greet him, bobbing proudly between his thin legs. Logan had to taste him. It felt like it had been ages since he'd tasted his mate. He dipped his head and sucked the bulbous tip into his mouth.

The noises streaming from Keeton's mouth made Logan feel like a king. Dropping his head further, he took his lover's cock to the back of his throat. He ran his tongue back and forth against the base of Keeton's shaft, swallowing again and again until Keeton began to hump his hips against Logan's face.

His fingers dug into Logan's scalp, pushing and pulling his head, fucking his mouth with abandon. Logan relaxed his throat muscles, clamped his lips tightly around the hard flesh in his mouth, and allowed his mate to set the pace. He kept one hand on his lover's hip, his other hand working frantically to undo his pants.

Logan pulled his pulsing cock free just as Keeton began to jerk and whimper. He fisted his own erection, stroking himself as Keeton tensed, and his lover's hot, bitter seed bathed his tongue and throat.

He swallowed quickly, not wanting to miss a drop of his mate's essence. Even when he had tapped Keeton for all he had, he continued to suck and tongue Keeton's cock until it began to fill and harden again.

"Logan, now. Oh, please fuck me!"

Releasing Keeton's renewed erection, Logan reached for the lube and quickly coated his fingers and throbbing cock. "Shh, angel, I'm going to take good care of you. Don't I always take care of you?"

His hand shook as he rimmed Keeton's clenching hole and pushed in with two fingers. He pumped in and out until Keeton relaxed enough for him to insert a third.

"Logan, I'm ready. Oh, damn, please!"

Removing his fingers, he positioned the weeping head of his dick against his lover's opening. "Deep breath, baby."

When Keeton sucked in a lungful of air, Logan pushed forward slowly, breaching his mate's snug entrance.

"Oh, fuck," he growled.

The heat and tightness of his mate's body surrounded him. The pleasure assaulted him, immediate and intense. Logan gripped the base of his cock to forestall his orgasm as he pumped just the tip in and out of his lover.

Keeton wrapped his small legs around Logan's hips and pulled with a strength that belied his small stature. Logan fell forward, Keeton's body swallowing his cock until his hand rested against the man's ass.

"Move your hand, love. We have all night," Keeton coaxed.

Reluctantly, he released his grip on his shaft and slid the rest of the way home. Keeton arched his back, moaning like a pro, the noises driving Logan wild. He'd never last with those happy little whimpers filling his ears, but he knew trying to keep his mate quiet only made him yell louder.

He slid an arm under Keeton's hips, lifting him to meet his thrusts. It would be a short, hard ride, but he'd make sure Keeton followed him over the edge.

Keeton wrapped his arms around Logan's neck, pulling himself up and pressing their chests together. His head fell back on his shoulders, his eyes drifting closed, and his full lips parting slightly. Sweat beaded across his creamy skin, glistening like diamonds in the moonlight.

"Claim me," he breathed.

Logan's already shaky control completely disintegrated. His hips jerked, and he plunged into his mate without restraint. Keeton's moans rose in volume, and he met Logan stroke for stroke, push for push. "So close. Do it, love." Keeton's eyes drifted closed again, and his head tilted to the side to bare his neck.

Zeroing in on the pulsing vein that snaked along Keeton's slender throat, Logan bent his head, licking at the salty flesh and sucking it into his mouth. His thrusts became erratic as his canines pushed through the soft skin, and Keeton's blood rushed over his tongue, flooding his mouth.

Keeton cried out, and Logan felt the sticky heat of his mate's release against his stomach. Logan pulled his canines from his lover's neck, threw his head back, and cried out to the moon.

His balls drew tight to his body, his lower belly clenched, and lightning zinged along his spine. One more hard thrust and Logan stilled, coating his mate's velvet-lined passage with his orgasm. The rhythmic tightening of Keeton's muscles prolonged his climax, rocking him to his core with its intensity.

Happy but exhausted, Logan gently pulled from his lover's body and collapsed beside him. "Wow," he panted.

"You can say that again." Keeton giggled. "Makeup sex rocks!"

Levering himself on one elbow, Logan smiled down at his mate.

"That wasn't makeup sex. That was engagement sex." He kissed the tip of Keeton's nose. "And we'll be having a lot more of it while you plan our wedding."

"How do you feel about a really long engagement?" Keeton smirked.

Chapter Twenty-One

"What the hell is going on?" Xander yelled, walking into the kitchen, shirtless, barefoot, and blurry-eyed.

Keeton glanced at the clock on the microwave and bit his lip. Two o'clock in the morning, and he and Braxton were shrieking like a couple of schoolgirls. "Sorry, Z-Dog," he apologized. "I didn't mean to wake you."

"Oh, phooey!" Braxton flicked his hand at Xander in dismissal. "You don't have to work until six o'clock Monday morning. Suck it up, bubba."

"Bubba?" Xander arched a brow at his mate and crossed his arms over his massive chest. "You do realize I'm more than twice your size in this form alone. And when I shift—"

"You're a big pussycat," Braxton cut him off. "Now hush. We're celebrating."

"Rather loudly," Xander agreed, nodding his head. "And, just what are you celebrating?"

"Keeton has agreed to marry me," Logan answered, beaming like a fool. He walked right up to Keeton and wrapped his arms around him snuggly.

Xander gaped at them. "Really? Wow!" His face broke into a huge grin, and he hurried over to thump Logan on the back. "Congratulations, brother!"

"I wish I was getting married," Braxton mumbled under his breath.

"Hey, I asked you to marry me, and you said no." Xander huffed indignantly.

"What? Why did you say no?" Keeton demanded.

Braxton snorted and rolled his eyes. "Please. Telling me that if we were 'hitched,'" Braxton made air quotations with his fingers, "your insurance premiums would go down, is not exactly a proposal of marriage. It sounds more like a Geico commercial."

Keeton looked up at Logan, over to Xander, blinked twice, and burst out laughing. "You did not!"

Xander blushed guiltily. "Kinda, yeah."

"Classic." Logan chuckled. "Very romantic, man. You do know that since your marriage wouldn't be legal in the state of Georgia, it would not affect your insurance premiums."

"Shut up," Xander groaned. He stared down at the floor for a long time, and when he looked up again, Keeton could see the determination blazing in his eyes. He knelt on both knees in front of Braxton, looking up at him with such open love and adoration, Keeton had to blink away tears.

"Braxton, you know I love you. I'm not good with words like Logan, but I promise I'll spend every day of our lives loving you. You're it for me, babe. It's just you and me, forever. Marry me?"

Rather than feeling like Braxton and Xander were cutting in on his moment, Keeton was ecstatic to share something so monumental with his best friend. They could have a double wedding. Thoughts spun into ideas, and ideas into plans, and Keeton could barely contain his excitement.

It suddenly dawned on him that Braxton hadn't said yes. He had yet to say anything. Looking away from Xander, he focused on his friend. Braxton's eyes bulged, and his mouth hung open. Unshed tears shimmered in his eyes, and his hand rested over his heart. If Keeton didn't know better, he'd think Braxton was having a stroke.

Biting his lip to keep from laughing, he nudged Braxton's shoulder with his own, shaking his friend from his stupor. "Say yes," he said around a smirk.

Braxton just nodded mutely. Xander's brows drew together in

concern, and he looked up at Keeton for help. "Does that mean he will marry me?" He turned back to Braxton. "Baby, are you okay? Say something."

"Yes," Braxton whispered, barely audible. He launched himself into Xander's lap and sobbed. "Yes, I will marry you," he wailed.

Xander held Braxton to his chest and rocked him side to side. "Why are you crying, *chulo*?"

"Because I'm so happy." Braxton hiccupped.

Keeton almost felt sorry for Xander. He looked so confused and bewildered, it was actually kind of comical.

"Don't worry. Keeton did the same thing," Logan assured his alpha. "He'll be fine in a minute."

Sure enough, seconds later, Braxton attacked Xander's mouth with an enthusiasm that was a little embarrassing to witness. Thankfully, Xander seemed to realize this and scooped his mate up, carrying him out of the room.

"Are you okay?" Logan asked, placing a kiss on the top of Keeton's head.

"Better than okay." Keeton smiled up at him. "I'm happy for them, and I'm happy for us. I don't need a celebration when I've already gotten the prize."

"The things you say," Logan whispered thickly. "Come on, angel. We'll have our own celebration." The next words came between nibbling kisses to Keeton's lips. "Our own...very private...celebration."

* * * *

The Fourth of July dawned hot and humid. By noon, the temperature climbed into the triple digits. Xander left at six that morning to begin his grueling twenty-four-hour shift. Logan received a call and left shortly afterward to fill in for a no-show. His own arduous twelve-hour shift becoming an eighteen-hour marathon.

Jackson and Talon decided to go fishing. Keeton wanted no part of that particular activity. Boston was spending the day with his newest squeeze, some little redheaded twink, from what Keeton understood. In fact, he hadn't seen much of the brother in the last couple of weeks.

Keeton waited under house arrest, of course. Only, his attitude had changed about the forced confinement. He now understood why Logan wanted him to stay home, and why it was important for Blaise to be within yelling distance at all times. Nothing had happened in several days, but less than thirty-six hours remained before the rise of the full moon.

Keeton could only imagine that Mariah's desperation climbed toward perilous levels. Something was coming, and the air sizzled with nervous anticipation. They needed a plan—quick, fast, and in a hurry.

"I think I've come up with a plan," Blaise announced as though he'd been picking Keeton's brain. "You're not going to like it." He frowned at him and shook his head seriously. "I don't know any other way, though."

"Will it stop that demon bitch, and will anyone get hurt?"

"Yes, I think it will stop her. I can't guarantee no one will be hurt, but it should be pretty safe."

"Then I'm on board." Logan would play a big part in this little ruse. Keeton didn't like it, but he knew what was at stake. "Logan's going to have to seduce her, right?"

Blaise's eyes rounded, but he nodded. "Not just him, though."

"Wait. What do you mean?" Braxton jumped to his feet and stomped toward Blaise. "My mate is not going to touch that filthy, soul-sucking whore!"

Blaise held up his hands defensively. "Braxton, will you please calm down? Xander isn't going to have to touch anyone."

Keeton rolled his eyes. Yeah, love made his friend *real* rational. "Braxton, sit your ass down and shut up. You want to stop her, right?

Well, then get over yourself and let's hear what Blaise has to say."

Braxton glared at him. "I don't like this," he grumbled, sitting on the love seat and crossing his arms over his chest.

Pacing the room and gesturing wildly, Blaise outlined his strategy to defeat Mariah Bernini. The plan sounded good. Simple and to the point, it seemed effective in theory.

Keeton didn't thrill to Logan's role in the scheme, or the fact that he would have to stay behind to wait and worry. Unfortunately, Logan's part in the plan constituted about ninety-percent of the total. The other ten percent sounded great, though.

"I don't like this," Braxton repeated his earlier complaint.

"Well, you don't exactly see me doing backflips either, honey." Keeton was becoming irritated with Braxton's negative attitude. "What's your problem anyway?"

"I'm scared, okay!" his friend shouted at him. "If something happens to Logan, I lose you, too! Excuse the fuck out of me for actually giving a shit about you!"

Keeton sat in silence as he watched Braxton flee from the room and up the stairs. He rubbed the back of his neck with one hand while pinching the bridge of his nose with the other. Could things get any worse?

"Keeton." Blaise paused until Keeton looked up at him. "Logan is going to have to sell this thing. He may have to take it further than you'd like."

Closing his eyes, he sighed audibly. Apparently, things could get worse.

Chapter Twenty-Two

Logan looked at his mate in astonishment. He had just arrived home after spending the day and most of the night in hell. He was exhausted, his head pounded, and his body ached. The last thing he wanted to discuss was seducing someone other than his mate.

"You want me to have sex with her?" Logan's brain might have been mush, but Keeton had taken complete leave of his senses.

"Oh, hell no! I don't care how gorgeous your ass is, I will kick it up one side and down the other if you have sex with that cow."

Logan stripped out of his sweat-crusted uniform and headed for the shower. "Baby, I'm tired, my head is going to split in two, and I just want to sleep. Can't this wait until tomorrow?"

He turned on the spray and brushed his teeth as he waited for the water to heat. Keeton followed him into the bathroom, but made no move to join him in the shower.

"I know, love, I do. And I'm sorry, but it really can't wait. The full moon is tomorrow night, and you're going to spend most of the day sleeping." Keeton jumped up to sit on the counter and sighed. "You have to arrange to meet with Mariah tomorrow before sunset."

Logan stepped into the shower and moaned as the hot water washed the last eighteen hours away. The water felt great, but his mattress called to him. He showered quickly, dried himself, and stumbled naked down the hall to his bedroom.

He climbed into bed, snuggled under the blankets, and reached for his mate. Keeton undressed quickly and slid in beside him.

"Come here, angel. God, you smell good." He held Keeton closely, breathing him in. "I can't think right now. Just let me sleep for a few hours, and then we'll talk. I promise."

"Fine," Keeton mumbled around a yawn as he snuggled in closer. "But this is important."

"Mm." Logan was already nodding off. Thank the powers that be he had the next three days off. "Lubya," he slurred.

Keeton giggled softly. "Love you, too,"

* * * *

"Well, hello, my sweet. And to what do I owe the pleasure?" Mariah's silky smooth voice set Logan's teeth on edge. He took a deep breath to calm his annoyance. *You can do this.*

"Hey, beautiful. I was wondering if we could talk somewhere private." He dropped his voice conspiratorially. "Somewhere away from Keeton."

A long pause preceded Mariah's voice before it drifted over the receiver. "Really? I can't help but think this is a trick."

Logan glanced over at his mate apologetically. He couldn't do what he needed to do, say what he needed to say, with Keeton in the room. Lying convincingly wouldn't be easy with his emotions tangled as they were.

Keeton seemed to understand without words. He nodded, blew Logan a silent kiss, and hurried out of the room.

"It's no trick." He sighed dramatically. The words that were about to come out of his mouth made him feel nauseous. "I can't stand him. You were right. He's obnoxious and needy, and making love to him is like fucking a corpse." Logan lowered his voice seductively. "I miss you, baby. I'm so sorry I let him come between us."

"Even though you know what I am now?" She still sounded uncertain and not completely convinced of his sincerity. He'd have to do better.

"Why should it matter to me what you are. You love me. I..." Logan almost choked on the next words, but powered through it, "love you. Nothing else matters. Besides, it beats being stuck with a *human*." He spat the word as if it left a bad taste in his mouth.

"You love me?" Mariah gasped. "Okay, I will meet you."

"Thank God," Logan breathed in relief. He didn't even have to fake it. "There's a small clearing in the western section of our woods. It'll be perfect for what I have planned for us. You know the one." He said it lightly, but inside, his blood boiled. It was the same clearing where Mariah had attacked Keeton. "Nice job, by the way."

"It was nothing." She laughed, proud and cocky. "He's so weak. I don't know what you ever saw in him anyway."

"You need to mate tonight, don't you, baby?"

"Yes," Mariah answered hesitantly. "Breeding will keep me strong for a long time." She clucked her tongue. "Hunting is so bothersome."

"Do you want to breed with me? Would you like that?" Logan choked back the bile that rose in his throat.

"Oh, your offspring would make me very strong," she sang excitedly. "I'm so glad you've finally come around. I would have bred with you tonight regardless, but it makes it so much easier when you cooperate."

Logan squeezed his eyes shut tightly and fought to keep his breathing even. "And if you bred with all of us?"

"Your pack would never agree to it, and I've run out of time. You'll have to do," she pouted.

"I think I can convince them. You won't hurt them, right? Just fuck them and send them on their way?"

"Of course. I just want their seed. I won't hurt them." He could hear the lie in her voice. "I want you though, Logan Cartwright," she purred. "You'll stay with me? You'll help me?"

"Help you?"

"Seek vengeance against my legion for shunning me." Mariah growled and hissed. "They dismissed me, tossed me away like garbage. They will pay."

"Why were you exiled?" Though it bore no real importance, Logan couldn't rein in his curiosity.

"The elders said my hunting habits garnered too much unwelcome attention to our legion." She huffed in exasperation. "It was just one little bitty orphanage."

Logan nearly choked. Acid churned in his stomach, boiling up his esophagus, making speech impossible.

"So, you'll help me? You and your pack would be a great asset to me."

"Anything you want, baby. I'll see you in the clearing at eight o'clock." He needed to get off the phone before he blew everything. "We can have our little reunion first." He let innuendo slip into his voice. "I will have my brothers meet us there a little later. We'll line up, bend you over that big rock, and fuck you like the slut that you are."

Mariah moaned loudly. "I'm all wet and waiting for you, Logan baby. I'll be there at eight."

Logan almost threw up in his mouth.

"Can't wait," he whispered. Ending the call, he just sat on his bed, staring at the closed door of his bedroom. He could hear Keeton on the other side. How long had he been there, and how much had he heard? The idea that Keeton believed a word of his conversation with Mariah made him ill.

"You can come in now, angel," Logan called to his mate. He heard Keeton yelp on the other side of the door, and he smiled, shaking his head.

The door eased open slowly, and Keeton smiled at him sheepishly. "Hi." The dead look in his eyes, the way his hands twisted together nervously, clued Logan in that he had heard most of the conversation.

He opened his arms and beckoned to him wordlessly. Keeton shuffled forward until he stood between Logan's parted knees. Placing his hands on his lover's hips, Logan looked up at him seriously.

"You know I didn't mean a word of that. You understand that I have to say what she wants to hear if this is going to work."

"I know," Keeton whispered. He looked at Logan for a long time, chewing on his bottom lip. Finally, he reached out, cupping Logan's face with both hands, and pressed a swift kiss to his lips. "Don't tell her that you love her again. That's all I ask…please."

"Promise," Logan answered immediately. He flipped his mate under him and pressed him into the mattress. "Anything else?" Without waiting for an answer, he attacked Keeton's mouth.

In six hours, he had to meet with the demon heifer. Logan would spend every one of them reassuring his mate how much he wanted, needed, and loved him.

But, Keeton pushed him away gently, and smiled. "I don't need this. I know you love me."

Logan kissed him again. To know that Keeton didn't question his love made him feel ten feet tall. "Then what would you like to do, angel?"

"Since we seem to be fairly safe for the time being…" He bit his lip and wrinkled his nose, looking too adorable for words. "Can we go out?" Keeton blurted. "I need to get my hair done and go shopping." He held his hand up, inspecting his fingers. "And my nail beds are gross right now. My eyebrows are in desperate need of waxing, and there is not a thing in this house for me to eat. Maybe we could go to dinner and see a movie if we have time?"

Logan laughed. It felt so good that he did it again. "Well, we can't have you walking around in old clothes, untreated hair, and misshapen brows." He patted Keeton's hip and rolled off of him. "Get dressed, baby."

Keeton looked like he had won the lottery. He stared at Logan, openmouthed, for a split second before his lips parted in a huge grin. Bounding from the bed, he crossed the room and dressed in record time. "Ready!" he announced. "Let's go!" He trembled like a

Chihuahua in his excitement.

Logan had no idea what he had gotten himself into, but anything that put that look on his angel's face was fine by him. He followed Keeton's sexy ass down the stairs and out to his Jeep.

"You know, you could use a trim as well, and maybe some highlights." Keeton leaned over and pushed Logan's hair back from his face as they pulled out of the drive and onto the main road. "We could get you a whole spa treatment! Oh, it will be so much fun!"

Logan gulped. He seriously doubted that.

Chapter Twenty-Three

Stepping through the trees and into the clearing, Logan found it completely deserted. He didn't like it. He had purposely arrived a few minutes late to avoid exactly this. He didn't like the idea of Mariah sneaking up on him.

Damn, it had been a long day. Keeton had drug him from store to store, shoving him into dressing rooms with armfuls of clothes. *"You dress like a hobo,"* Keeton said as he shook his head sadly. *"Your closet is in desperate need of a makeover."*

Then Keeton insisted Logan needed a haircut. He had even reluctantly agreed to add a few highlights. He was tense and nervous through the whole process, but had to admit, he looked damn good.

He had drawn the line at having anything waxed, plucked, buffed, or polished. Instead, he'd sat in a relaxing steam room while Keeton had all those things done. They both agreed that even though Logan couldn't smell Mariah, she could smell him, and he'd need to purge most of Keeton's scent. After all, he was supposed to despise his little mate.

After the steam room, and Keeton's many body-beautifying treatments, his lover had talked him into a couple's massage. He'd had to bite his lip several times to keep from moaning out loud. It had been amazing, and his body felt wonderful.

There hadn't been time for a movie, but they did grab a quick bite on the veranda of a quaint little diner. Keeton claimed the place had the best manicotti in town. He'd been correct.

His already gorgeous mate looked too tempting to be legal after his day at the spa. Logan vowed to start a fund for his lover to go at least once a week. Unfortunately, he now had a hard time keeping his hands to himself. More than once, Keeton had to remind him that there could be no loving until after the pack remedied their little demon dilemma.

Electricity zipped along his spine as darkness crept into the clearing. The sun slowly sank toward the horizon, moonrise less than an hour away. He only needed to stall for twenty minutes or so, and then his brothers would be there, ready to have his back.

"Well, hello, Logan," Mariah purred as she stepped into the clearing. "Should we just forego the pleasantries and get right down to business?"

The sleeves of her bloodred silk shirt billowed in the breeze. The black leather pants and matching corset molded to her like a second skin. She propped one foot up on the rock beside her and began to unzip her knee-high boots. "Or did you want a little appetizer before the main course?"

Logan had discussed the boundaries with Keeton before he set out for the forest. His lover understood how far Logan would have to take his seduction. All he requested was no sex—oral or otherwise.

"What type of appetizer did you have in mind, my pretty?" Crap, she did absolutely nothing for him. She would be able to smell his lack of interest long before she realized he wasn't getting hard.

"Well, I could suck you. I seem to remember how much you like that. No coming, of course. We have to save your seed."

No. "What about a little striptease? Let me see what I've been missing." He sauntered up to Mariah and yanked her to him. "Let me see that gorgeous body," he whispered heavily into her ear.

She leaned away, grinning seductively, as she trailed her fingers down to the top button of his jeans and flicked it open. Hate bubbled up inside of him, and he had to fight the urge to stop her. His zipper yielded to her touch, his jeans parting to reveal his closely cropped curls. She smiled in satisfaction, then pushed him roughly away.

He fell back onto the rock she had rested her foot on with a grunt.

Leaning casually against the boulder behind him, Logan stared up at his ex-girlfriend. Had he really thought her beautiful? She looked more like a velociraptor, and that was *before* her demon shift.

"I want to watch, too. I'll strip, you play." She nodded toward his groin for emphasis.

Logan didn't say a word. He pushed his pants down far enough to reach inside and pull out his flaccid cock. Mariah frowned at him. "Well, that just won't do, will it?" She started to dance and sway around him, slowly pulling at the strings of her corset. "Don't worry, my sweet. I know just how to fix that."

* * * *

Keeton paced the living room, running his fingers through his hair, and completely destroying his new styling. The pack had just left to meet Logan, and Keeton couldn't control his nervous worry.

"This had better work." He pointed a finger at his cousin.

"It will. Relax, Keeton, and sit down. You're making me nervous."

"Shut up," Keeton and Braxton said in unison. Braxton had emerged from the kitchen to pace alongside him.

"I can't do this." He stopped abruptly and spun toward the front door. "I have to be there."

"The hell you do!" Blaise yelled as he sprang up from the floor. "You are not going anywhere. Not only is it not safe, but Logan would hand me my ass. I'm rather fond of that particular part of my anatomy, so just sit down."

Keeton glanced over at his best friend. "I'm coming, too," Braxton said promptly.

"Oh, no, you're not!" Blaise's face turned so red, Keeton worried he would pop a blood vessel. "You two can just get that out of your head right now. You. Are not. Leaving!"

"Blaise, I can't just sit here and do nothing," Keeton pleaded.

"He's my mate!"

"I know." Blaise's voice softened marginally. "But, it's not safe. Not only are you free game for Mariah, but you can't be around the others when they shift. You know that." He turned to Braxton. "Same goes for you, Brax."

"I don't care," Keeton stated vehemently. "Haven't you ever loved someone so much that it didn't matter? So much that you would do anything to keep them safe, no matter the risks?"

Blaise frowned at him, but didn't answer. *Apparently not.* Keeton found that kind of sad. "Forget it." Blaise shook his head. "It's not going to happen. I don't care how much you beg, I'm bigger than both of you, and you're not leaving this—oomph."

His eyes rolled back in his head, and he crumpled to the floor. Braxton stood behind him, holding one of the table lamps. "Right, sorry about that," he mumbled down at Blaise. "Let's go." He dropped the lamp and started toward the door.

Keeton grabbed him by the arm and whirled him around. "Are you sure? You know what the risks are."

Braxton glared at him, his hands fisted on his hips. "My mate is out there, too. If you think I'm staying behind, you don't know me at all. You can try to stop me and you'll get the same treatment as Blaise."

Keeton grinned. "Just making sure. Come on, we have to hurry."

* * * *

Logan stroked his cock, trying to bring it to life. Mariah was already half naked, her breasts fully exposed, and he still remained limp. He'd never had this problem before, especially not with Keeton. All that creamy skin and lean muscle had him standing at attention in no time flat.

The thought of his mate had Logan's cock twitching. He felt a little wrong thinking about Keeton in his current situation, but he would have to go with it. Staring at Mariah, his mind mapped the contours of his lover's body—the flat expanse of his stomach, the gentle curve of his hips, and the pulsing hardness of his gorgeous prick.

He stroked faster as his cock began to fill and thicken. Hopefully, Mariah wouldn't notice the blank, faraway look in his eyes. Pictures of Keeton, wanton, needy, and writhing in passion beneath him, flickered by like an old movie. All thoughts of Mariah floated away as the erotic images of his mate continued to bombard him.

Then, Mariah stopped dancing and lifted her head to sniff the air. "Ah, our guests have arrived." Her mouth split into a wide, predatory grin.

Logan almost sighed in relief. He quickly jumped up and began stripping off his clothes. Mariah eyed him appreciatively. "Eager to get started, I see."

"You have no idea," Logan answered honestly. He wanted to get this over with in the worst way.

Mariah's body jerked back, her eyes narrowing into slits. "Deceiver!" she hissed. Her claws extended, and she slashed away the remainder of her clothing.

Logan could feel the power in the air around them. He could feel the call of the moon, and the added pull from his pack's magic. He couldn't shift yet, though. The muscles in his neck corded as the beast within him strained to free itself from its confinement. *Just a little longer*.

Talon and Jackson stepped through the trees first. The sleek snow leopard and the handsome white wolf took up ranks to the right. Next through the trees came Boston. The huge white stag looked almost ethereal in his beauty. He stepped to the left and pawed the ground with his hooves. Xander appeared last and stood in the middle, still in human form.

Once Logan saw his alpha, he sprinted toward Boston, hitting the ground beside the stag and shifting in record time. He looked across to his twin, a mirror image of himself, and nodded. Talon nodded back, then returned his attention to the demon in front them.

Mariah had completely transformed. Her skin, that sickly gray color, her eyes coal black, and blue veins snaked across her entire body. She opened her mouth and hissed, revealing rows of razor-sharp daggers. She stumbled toward them, spitting and yowling.

Logan's heart raced inside his chest. It wasn't working. They needed more magic to push her to the breaking point. If Xander shifted, that left no one with opposable thumbs to subdue her, though. Blaise had made them promise to try to take her alive.

Logan agreed. He didn't want anyone to die tonight, but if it came down between them or her, he wouldn't hesitate to rip her slimy throat out.

A familiar scent caught his attention, and he inhaled deeply, his eyes darting about the trees. *No!*

Fuck, he was going to flog Blaise bloody.

Chapter Twenty-Four

Keeton ducked behind a tree and peeked around. Braxton huddled close behind him, peering over his shoulder. "Gross," he breathed in Keeton's ear.

He had a point. Mariah looked like something straight from a Wes Craven movie. She snarled and shrieked as her body jerked and twisted. Two little nubs on her back pulsed just above her shoulder blades. With horror, Keeton realized her wings were trying to break through. If she succeeded, they might as well just roll over and die.

She stumbled forward in gruesome, halting movements that he compared to zombies. Keeton could see the pack across the clearing, but he didn't know if Logan was the leopard on the left or the right. Both looked exactly the same. Then he realized the one on the left stared right at him. *Fucking wonderful.*

"Logan knows we're here," he whispered to Braxton.

Before Braxton could reply, all hell broke loose. Mariah's wings burst from her back, and she launched herself at Xander. Jackson came flying out of nowhere, barking and snarling, colliding with Mariah midair, just feet from Xander.

Braxton scrambled from the brush and took off at a dead run. "Xander, shift!" he screamed over and over as he sprinted across the clearing.

"Shit." Keeton sprinted toward the action, chasing his best friend. Whatever happened, they were in this together.

* * * *

Logan hissed and growled as he slashed at Mariah's leathery wings with his claws. They couldn't let her get airborne. A hand connected with his head, and he felt himself flying through the air. Thank God that tree had been there to break his fall. He bounced off the tree trunk and rolled to a stop twenty feet from the brawl. Damn, that bitch packed a punch.

Getting to his feet, he shook his head to clear it.

"Xander, shift!"

Logan jerked his head up to see Braxton and Keeton sprinting across the clearing and groaned internally. If Mariah didn't kill them, he would.

A ripple of power washed through him, inducing a shudder. He didn't have to look to know that Xander had shifted...and his alpha was pissed. The four-hundred-pound white tiger leapt through the air, knocking Mariah to the ground and pinning her under his massive paws.

Logan crept closer, his muscles still tense and prepared for battle. He'd experienced Mariah's strength firsthand.

Keeton rushed up to him and dropped to his knees, running his hands over Logan's fur. He stared at him in terror when his right hand came away bloody. "You're hurt."

If he could, he would have rolled his eyes. Yeah, he was hurt. His left side ached and burned like hell. Instead, Logan rubbed his head against Keeton's chest and neck. He'd be mad at his mate later. Right now, he was just too thankful that his angel was unharmed.

A loud shriek, followed by an even louder roar, drew Logan's attention. He turned toward the commotion, positioning himself between his mate and any danger. Mariah had flipped Xander, and she sat on top of him, making bloodied ribbons out of his chest and side.

Everyone was hurt. Jackson lay on the ground, unmoving. Boston tried in vain to push to his feet, but fell back to the ground with an unholy sound escaping his mouth.

Talon was limping and bloody, but he still managed to leap onto

Mariah's back and sink his teeth into her neck. She screeched, pausing in her assault on Xander long enough to reach over her head with both hands and catapult Talon through the air. He landed several feet away and didn't get back up.

"She's lost her mind," Keeton whispered. "You've pushed her to insanity, but some people only get crazy strong when they reach that point."

Logan hadn't thought of that. No one had, but Keeton was right. Instead of weakening, Mariah seemed to be gaining in strength.

He turned to look right into Keeton's eyes. Logan hoped his mate understood what he had to do. He probably wouldn't survive it, but he couldn't just stand there and watch his friend, his brother, die.

Keeton nodded as he wiped away a tear. "I know. I love you, Logan. Go."

He nuzzled against Keeton's neck one last time, then turned and sprinted at his ex, his eyes locked on to her throat. That's where he needed to strike, and he'd only get one shot at it.

Mariah's attention snapped toward him, and she grinned, flicking her tongue. "Here kitty, kitty," she rasped.

"Braxton, no!" Keeton screamed.

Logan pulled up short, skidding to a stop, when Mariah grunted and fell over on her side with a heavy thud. Braxton stood above her, tears streaming down his face, and a huge rock held above his head. He brought it down over Mariah's head again as he yelled and sobbed.

"You fucking bitch! I hope you rot in Hell!"

Keeton pushed past Logan and tackled his friend to the ground. He sat on Braxton's chest and pinned his shoulders to the dirt. "Braxton, stop! Snap out of it! You did it, honey. You did it."

* * * *

Night had fallen. The moonlight the only thing illuminating the clearing as Keeton grinned down at Braxton. His friend really needed to deal with his anger issues and stop bashing people over the head with inanimate objects.

Just this one time, he wouldn't complain, though.

Keeton's grin quickly slid from his face when Braxton's head began whipping from side to side, and his body jerked and bucked beneath him. Then the screams began. The sounds coming from his best friend chilled Keeton's blood. His hands clawed frantically at the ground, and he panted and sobbed out Xander's name in between shrieks.

Keeton grabbed Braxton's head and held it still. "Logan, help me!" he yelled for his mate.

Logan was at his side in an instant, hovering over Braxton. *"He needs to block out the pain. He has to get his blood into Xander, or they're both going to die."*

Keeton looked at Logan as he struggled to control his friend. He had just heard Logan in his head. "Something you forgot to tell me?"

Logan jerked back, and his yellow eyes widened. *"I didn't know. Holy shit!"*

Keeton shook his head. "Later." Turning back to Braxton, he took a deep breath. "Sorry about this, honey." Then he doubled up his fist, reached back, and punched his best friend of forever square in the jaw.

Braxton's body stilled beneath him, and his eyes focused on Keeton. "You hit me," he accused. Then his eyes began to lose focus, and his muscles tensed again.

"And I'll do it again. You have to fight it, Braxton."

His eyes rolled back in his head, and his feet began to beat against the ground.

"Fight it, Braxton!" Keeton yelled. "If you can't control it, Xander is going to die! You both will," he added quietly.

Those seemed to be the magic words. Braxton's eyes flew open, and he struggled to push Keeton off of him. "Move, damn it," he demanded.

Keeton rolled off and watched him race to Xander. The alpha looked in bad shape. Blood matted his beautiful fur, standing out in sharp relief against the white of his pelt.

Braxton stroked a hand over his lover's face as tears streamed down his cheeks. He looked around frantically as if searching for something, then up at Logan, his eyes pleading. "Logan, help me. I need you to cut me."

Logan walked over to him and raised his left paw. Braxton held out his arm and nodded. Logan slashed a claw across his wrist, and blood flowed freely from the gash. Braxton never flinched.

"Thank you," he whispered before turning to Xander. He frowned and looked up at Keeton.

Keeton saw the problem immediately. He hurried over to the huge tiger and pulled his mouth open wide. He sighed in relief when Xander's warm breath washed over his hands and arms. Shallow and ragged, but still, Xander breathed.

Braxton positioned his bleeding wrist over Xander's mouth and squeezed with his other hand to encourage the flow. After several minutes, Keeton became concerned. Xander breathed easier, and the bleeding had stopped. Braxton, on the other hand, grew paler by the second.

"That's enough," he said. He let go of Xander's massive jowls and reached for Braxton. "Braxton, that's enough. He's healing."

Braxton shook his head. "No, he needs more. He's hurting. I can feel it."

"Logan, do something." Keeton tried not to panic when Braxton swayed, and his eyelids drooped.

"Give him Xander's blood. I cut him pretty deep, but the blood will close the wound."

Keeton wrinkled his nose and smeared his fingers in the blood on Xander's chest. Then he slapped Braxton across the face with an open hand. When Braxton gasped, Keeton shoved two fingers into his friend's open mouth. Braxton choked and gagged, but swallowed convulsively.

The blood flow stopped immediately as the wound began to heal itself. Braxton stared at it in distress. "No," he whispered. Then he stretched out on the ground, cuddled close to Xander, and cried. The sounds of his sobs broke Keeton's heart. He watched Braxton nuzzle his face against Xander's cheek and stroke his fingers through the thick fur on his mate's neck.

Keeton moved away slowly and walked toward Mariah's unconscious body. Logan was there in a flash, blocking Keeton's way and pushing against his legs. *"She's not dead, and you are not going anywhere near her,"* he growled inside Keeton's head.

Dropping to his knees, he took Logan's furry face in both hands. His mate looked so gorgeous in his leopard form, and his fur felt silky soft. "I know she's not dead." He could see the red and orange of her aura pulsing around her, the core still as black as the night. "We need to tie her up though, and I seem to be the only one with thumbs that's not emotionally distraught at the moment. I'll be fine, love."

"I don't like it. Hurry and tie her, but if she so much as twitches, I will rip her throat out."

"Fair enough," Keeton sighed. He kissed Logan's nose and stood. "So, did you guys think to bring rope?"

Chapter Twenty-Five

Wednesday was a test in patience. With everyone banged up from the fight, they all acted like a bunch of toddlers as far as Keeton was concerned. Even Blaise moped about, moaning and complaining that his head was going to explode.

"Oh, just man up, already!" Keeton yelled. Everyone winced, and Talon and Blaise grabbed their heads.

"Logan, can't you do something with him?" Jackson whined from the couch. He rested against several pillows with Talon's feet nestled in his lap. "He's like Barbie on steroids, man."

Logan wrapped his arms around Keeton from behind and pressed a soft kiss to the side of his neck. Keeton shivered and wiggled against his mate. "Keeton and Braxton saved our asses last night. I'd think you would be a little more grateful."

"And just how is that?" Boston asked as he hobbled into the room. His right leg had been broken in the fray. It was mending, but he said it would still be a few days before it completely healed. "Why are they not drooling and scribbling outside of the lines with washable crayons right now?"

"Obviously they're both Moonlighters," Logan answered. "Though, one thing still bothers me. The chances of you both being part of the breed are practically nonexistent. Blaise?"

Keeton looked over at his cousin and raised a brow in question. "Do you know something?"

Blaise groaned. "Not really, but I have a theory." He rose from the couch and led them toward the stairs. "Braxton needs to hear this, too, and demons couldn't pull him from Xander's side right now."

Keeton rolled his eyes. "Not funny, man." He followed his cousin up the stairs with Logan trailing behind.

"Do you want me to wait in our room?" Logan asked when they reached Braxton and Xander's door.

"No, of course not," Keeton answered immediately.

He knocked softly, then pushed the door open without waiting for a reply. Logan had given Xander something to help him sleep while he healed, and the big alpha rested in bed, a slight frown on his lips. Keeton remembered the small dose of poison from Mariah's bite, and he winced in sympathy at the pain Xander must be feeling.

Braxton walked out of their private bathroom, rubbing a towel across his head. "Hey, guys, what's up?"

To Keeton's relief, Braxton's color had returned, and he looked healthy, though tired. "How's Xander?"

Braxton smiled a little. "He's hurting, of course." He rubbed absently at his own chest. "We both are, but he's going to be fine. He just needs to rest." He looked at each man in the room. "What's going on?"

"Well, apparently, my dear cousin is going to tell us why we're not mumbling to the voices in our heads or drawing alien symbols on the ceilings. "

"Yeah, I was kind of wondering about that. I assume that means we are both dormant white shifters, but the odds seem pretty slim."

"It's possible, but not likely. We don't know much about the Moonlight Breed, and most of the information we do have is just hearsay and legend." Blaise shook his head in frustration. "Obviously, we can't do a lot of research. We can't get near them," he waved a hand at Logan, "you, when you shift. We can't do any studies." He was off on a soapbox.

"Is he going to get to the point anytime soon?" Braxton whispered to Keeton.

"I doubt it. Next comes the speech about life lessons and responsibilities."

"…and it's important for us to discover these things to better the lives of the preternatural population. It is our responsibility…" Blaise paced the room, waving his arms wildly, his voice rising.

"Told you," Keeton mumbled.

"Goody, because I was so afraid I'd miss this part." Braxton rolled his eyes and sighed. "Do you think we could wrap it up?"

Blaise halted in the middle of the room and glared at them. "Fine," he huffed. "I don't know for certain, and there is no way to test my theory." He grumbled about that for another few seconds. "Anyway, I think it is possible that not only can you be near your own mate when he shifts, but any other member of the breed as well. It's the only thing that makes sense."

Keeton shrugged. "It sounds good to me."

Braxton grinned and shrugged as well. "Whatever, man."

Blaise threw his hands in the air and growled. "That's all you have to say?"

"What else is there to say?" Logan spoke for the first time. "They're safe, and that's all that matters."

"I hate you all," Blaise groused and stomped from the room.

"What's his problem?" Logan asked before placing a kiss on Keeton's cheek.

"He's a diva. We didn't hang on his every word, so he's throwing a hissy fit."

"I heard that!" Blaise called from down the hall.

Everyone laughed.

* * * *

"It's been a pretty eventful weekend for you, angel." Logan sprawled naked across the bed as he watched his mate undress. Damn, his baby looked good. Logan's cock sprang to life, hardening between his legs.

"You can say that again. I hate to see Blaise go, though. I hope he doesn't stay gone so long this time."

Blaise travelled back to The Council to deliver the Arsidian Demon, Mariah Bernini. It so happened that Xander had brought rope with him into the clearing. Keeton did a marvelous job binding her, and Logan helped him drag her through the woods to the edge of the backyard. He had returned to his pack while Keeton went to rouse Blaise.

Blaise then gave Mariah a specially designed sedative, powerful enough to keep her more or less comatose for seventy-two hours.

Keeton climbed up on the bed between Logan's spread thighs and grinned. "Need some help with that?" He smirked at Logan's burgeoning erection.

"There seems to be quite a bit of swelling," Logan agreed. "What would you recommend?"

Keeton opened his mouth and dove forward to envelop Logan's cock. Logan groaned as his hips arched up off of the bed. "I love the way you think, baby."

Keeton chuckled around the turgid flesh in his mouth, sending faint vibrations along his shaft. Logan ground his teeth together and let his head drop back as his lover lavished attention on him. It felt like heaven. The only thing he loved more than Keeton's mouth...

He pushed Keeton's head back until his cock slid from his mouth with a naughty slurp. "What?" Keeton demanded.

Logan pulled Keeton to him, flipping him over and pressing his face into the mattress. "Ass up and spread your legs," he growled. He was way past self-control.

Luckily, Keeton seemed to be right there with him. He spread his thighs and pushed his ass in the air, wiggling it insistently. Logan gave it a sharp smack, then leaned over to lick away the sting.

Keeton's moans sounded muffled against the blankets. "Turn your head to the side, baby. I want to hear you scream tonight." Logan ran both hands over the perfect mounds of his lover's ass, then parted the cheeks to reveal his pretty pink pucker. "You waxed," he whimpered.

Logan wet his lips before leaning in to lick a wide swipe down his mate's crease. The scent and taste was completely Keeton, and it drove Logan wild. He licked and sucked, rimming his lover like a starving man.

Keeton pushed back against his face, moaning and panting. Logan pulled away to admire the shine of his mate's entrance. He ran one finger around the tight muscles, and slipped it in to the first knuckle. Keeton's hole sucked his finger in like a vortex.

Logan couldn't wait any longer. He stretched his mate quickly and reached for the lube on the nightstand. After slicking himself, he dribbled a little extra down Keeton's crease and eased his weeping prick inside, sheathing himself to the root.

Keeton yelled out in pleasure, pushing back against him, his hungry ass eating up Logan's length. The air rushed from Logan's lungs in a loud groan. "Ready, angel? It's going to be hard and fast."

"Fuck me," Keeton panted.

"Put your legs on the outside of mine."

He wiggled around until his ankles lay on the outside of Logan's knees and pushed back to signal his readiness. Logan pulled back slowly, one hand on Keeton's hip and the other between his mate's shoulders, and shoved back in forcefully.

He rode his mate hard, pumping into him faster and harder. Keeton mewled, moaned, and whimpered, but Logan wanted him screaming. He reached beneath his lover's damp body, fisted Keeton's leaking cock, and stroked him in time with his thrusts. Repositioning, he moved closer, pulling Keeton's ass higher, and nailed his sweet spot on the next plunge.

Keeton screamed.

His body tensed, and his inner muscles contracted in a strangle hold on Logan's dick. Hot, sticky cum erupted over Logan's hand and wrist as Keeton continue to scream out his release.

Logan thrust twice more, stilled, and yelled as his climax ripped through him. He pumped spurt after spurt of his hot seed deep into his lover's silky channel.

He dropped his head against his mate's back and waited for his breathing to return to normal. After several minutes, he pulled gently from Keeton's body and rolled onto his back beside him. "I needed that," he croaked hoarsely.

Keeton giggled and turned to face him. "I can see that. Your aura looks so much better." He kissed Logan's nose then rolled from the bed. Pulling Logan's shirt over his head, he hurried from the room and down the hall. A few minutes later, he returned with a warm, wet washcloth.

Logan took the cloth and cleaned himself quickly, throwing it in the direction of the hamper when he had finished. Keeton rolled his eyes, walked over to pick it up off the floor, and dropped it in the hamper.

"We really need to work on your domestic skills. You're not a leopard. You are a pig."

"Wow. Well, don't hold back, babe. Tell me how you really feel."

Keeton grinned and shook his head as he slid into the bed, snuggling up close to Logan. He nuzzled his face against Logan's chest, humming happily. "Oh, I promise you, no more holding back."

Logan wrapped his arms around his mate and sighed contentedly. "Happy to hear it, angel. I'm so glad I found you. I can't even imagine my life without you."

"Ditto," Keeton mumbled drowsily. "Now hush so I can sleep."

Logan laughed quietly and kissed his mate's blond head. He had walked into hell to face a demon and came out on the other side with an angel.

THE END

www.gabrielleevans.com

ABOUT THE AUTHOR

Gabrielle Evans grew up in a small town in southern Oklahoma. We're talking one red light that may or may not work depending on the day of the week. She married her high school sweetheart and the rest is pretty much history. They have two very active boys and one high-strung wiener dog that keeps her constantly on the go. For now, Gabrielle parks her car in north-central Texas, but who knows what tomorrow will bring.

Gabrielle believes in love at first sight and taking chances. She enjoys dreaming up and watching ideas come to life that push the boundaries of "normal" society. When she's not writing, she can usually be found testing those same boundaries.

Also by Gabrielle Evans

Siren Classic: The Moonlight Breed 1: *Leap of Faith*
Ménage Amour: Wicked River 1: *Keeper of the Light*

Available at
BOOKSTRAND.COM

Siren Publishing, Inc.
www.SirenPublishing.com

CPSIA information can be obtained at www.ICGtesting.com

263559BV00005B/63/P

9 781610 344777